The Gospel of Satan

Nicholas Fillmore

iambic Books

First paperback edition April 2023

Library of Congress Control Number: 2022919413

ISBN 979-8-218-09241-2 (paperback)
ISBN 979-8-218-09242-9 (ebook)

Printed in the U.S.A.

published by iambic Books
Honolulu, Hawaii
www.iambicbooks.com

ĭá

for Katharine and Elnora

Der tayvl iz nit azoy shvartz vi men molt im.
(The devil is not so black as we paint him.)
—Yiddish Proverb

Contents

The
Gospel
of
Satan

"Pleased to
Meet You"

I have one of those faces you think you've seen before, on CNN or a Ferragamo ad somewhere, vaguely Mediterranean, hungry, *ugly-sexy* I believe is the expression.

(Actually, I appear differently to everyone, not because of any ethereal quality—I *am* angelic—but some earthly notion of perfection. That is how He made me, or rather made *you*—to perceive me.

(As for *sexy*, we cherubim are famously chaste, sexless actually—*O che sciagura d'essere senza coglione!*—which probably accounts for a lot.

That's the first of three great secrets I'll share: our interrelation. See, we are not the same, but rather *of* the same.— And yet the same, for all that....

I've gone slumming in human affairs, having lost interest in divine. Heaven's a drag. (So's hell, obviously.) Either way, I'm here in this happy median. And I'll tell you what: my ambition is not to poach souls. (Yes, I have contracts: 111,157 as we speak, and I'm exclusive.) I do not desire to destroy kings, queens, mothers, maidens, priests. Well, priests is another matter. And lead singers.... Christ, our only real desire was to be human; to live such lives as we are able to live in this great, riotous disease-ridden world, free; to participate in art and love and death and all those things we cannot do for ourselves. Why else do you suppose He made you if not to escape *His* own hell? Now He hogs all the credit for Himself. *His* David. *His* Tenth. Check *my* IMBD; I've got a few credits: half of 70s cinema, a symphony or two, most of abstract expressionism.

Give me a dirge, a messy divorce, a smashed pot.…
How I love the human gaze: the alarm of mortal
recognition: the shocked look of a schoolgirl who's
turned to meet the eyes of an obvious roué. See me
and turn away.

—*You*, I see, have turned back, excellent fellow.

No, I don't believe we've met. Call me Lucifer.
Less formally, Satan.

Yes, that very one. Poacher of souls. Tempter
of Eve. (I'm also the author of your freedom, let's
not forget, without whom you'd still be puttering
around Eden.… But let me stop myself. If I have a
fault.…)

A drink? Of course. Why not? I know a place.

A Blue Note

Ah, a bar. Mid-town. 3PM. Hour of bad ideas, broken vows, suicides.— See those two down at the end? One will be dead tonight. It's true! It's true…. And what would I do about it? Do you suppose it's easy to overhear the sum total of human misery, this catalog of human sorrows, crammed in one's ears? Calumny, lust, stupidity, greed, hate? And love, nobility and reason, too….

But I am no Greek, content to amuse myself with Greek things. Nor some Jewish fantasy of retribution. I am something else entirely, which I fully intend to make you feel.

And you, my excellent fellow, wait, don't tell … an accountant … in publishing. A modern tale, indeed. And you want to write. More specifically to publish your own stories. For who hasn't a tale to tell? Oh, you are a fool, my friend— *Pagliaccio! Buffone! Clown!*— and yet, I'll admit, one with courage enough to laugh in His face—no lover of literature. Why, I've seen him rage a whole day because he was slighted. Unleash tidal waves, plagues.— (Perhaps I *am* interested.)

"Barkeep, Crown, neat."

(Oh, what a world.)

And what do you want from me? A little magic with the P&L? But that's your line, isn't it? Talent, then? That can be arranged—though hardly a prerequisite. You wouldn't believe how horribly all these rock stars squawk. Jagger? Pfft. Plant? Oif. Not a voice in the house. All it takes is a minor invention. A dash of genius, which is really nothing more than an act of will, contrary to the usual notion of artistic inspiration. I supply that.

Look, nobody wanted to listen to Robert Johnson droning on until I gave him that little turnaround. That's it. A trick is all. A gimmick.— Or *gesture*, if you prefer. Believe me, I'm no philistine. I just get bored, then want to break the mold.

Do you know where I first discovered that about myself? Why, my own personal crossroads, the heavenly *fucking* choir, of course.

Te Deum? Tedium!

All day matins through vespers we heaped praises on the divine (read Creator). In the beginning that was alright. Morning dissolved into midday, song built upon song and we sang, guided by an invisible score inscribed upon our hearts. (Don't all stories of family dysfunction begin this way?) Then a notion crept into my brain during an idle moment. Just a little alteration, a mere quartertone. And having thought of it, how could I resist? Of course there are those earnest amongst us for whom everything is a straight path. Deviation's the Devil's work. And those for whom the absurdity of our lives—they are absurd, no?—demands an equal show of absurdity. Humor is ontological, my friend, as the poet said. I flattened the note. Right there in the middle of Handel.

All of a sudden there was a great rushing about our ears, like the beating of wings, and a deafening roar as the Almighty descended upon us with his iron rod. He pitched a fucking fit! Tossed me headlong into an abyss along with five or six others with the effrontery to snigger.

Down. Down. I fell for eight days and nights not caring where I might land. You may think me rather *raffiné;* back then I was a mere child, disowned by his father, cast out, affrighted. I fell for eight days and on the ninth for mere boredom arrested my fall and curved in a long arc over the void until I saw something down below me, you can guess what.

I was lonely. I wanted company, and there, sitting upon a rock in leaf-shadow, was a creature of such exquisite, unaffected beauty you'd have thought she sprang from *His* rib rather than Adam's.— That's not how He works, of course. With Him everything's by innuendo, like a mafia don.

I sidled up to her as she sat there upon her rock.

"You-who," I called as matily as I might.

She started....

"Oh dear, I've frightened you ... Satan, if you please," I said, drawing near and reaching with trembling hand to arrange a stray lock of hair.

Still nothing. A rather dull conversationalist, actually.

"Coo-coo," I ventured.

A fugitive darkness passed over her face.

"Cluck-cluck?"

… Then she opened her mouth. You know the feeling, I take it my friend, of being spurned? "My husband," she pronounced in disgustingly maritorious tones, "is gathering water."

"So much the worse for him," I muttered through clenched teeth.

"Pardon me?" she said, regaining a measure of self-possession—another fucking trophy-wife in a Mercedes.

After that scene with Eve I climbed a hill outside Paradise…. Ahh, fuck it.— 'Stories,' you said, right? Give me fifty pages and I'll put together a pitch. I don't care what. We immortals don't set much store by your words, anyway, having read certain accounts. Your bible, for one, fucked things up pretty well, and that meddlesome fool, St. Paul, with his thumb prints all over the good part. (We'll get to Jesus.— I'll say *his* name, a *mensch* alright, but not his father's. No….)

A Blue Note

After that scene with Eve, I climbed a hill outside Paradise. Afternoon sun struck white outcrop-
pings, the blue Mediterranean lay flat as a stone.
Loathe to lift my eyes to heaven I searched the
ground. There, wreathed in thorns: I tore apart that
choke and ate its raw heart, throat burning, hot
tears pouring down my face, and spoke his name a
last time, swallowing that hateful syllable.

Witches

Here's the thing, though: It's amazing what a good night's sleep will do. That much we learned from you: your marvelous capacity for sleep. And in no time I'd forgotten my troubles and was zipping along like my old self.

Who can live like that, anyway, with hate in his heart 24/7? *Not I, said the rat.* Hate's a momentary passion, not a guiding principle. Milton got that part wrong—though one likes the jingle, "what matters if I be what I am, and what I should be."

As a matter of fact, I don't hate anything. Okay, maybe someone cuts you off in traffic. So next chance you cut them off and shoot them *il dito*. That's it. There's no real principle involved, unless you're some kind of psycho. Unless you're some kind of moralist. Unless you've got some kind of *philosophy.*

Admittedly, I've meddled in human affairs. Salem? Sure, I had a hand in that, only to see wither man's imagination might lead.

Camped on a frozen swamp at the edge of a great unknown, the Puritans hardly suspected their worst fears lay bolted behind their own front doors. (Moralists to the nth degree.) Yes, I visited Mercy Lewis, Abigail Williams, Ann Putnam—good girls with good Puritan names—and scandalized their dreams with visions of cock. Great horse cocks 'neath rearing stallions, bent old-man cocks, winged death's head cocks. Those girls were cock-crazy, all night in narrow beds with hands between their knees. The Puritan fathers were quick to put an end to that; hauled everyone they had a grievance with before the court—outspoken women, political rivals, slaves—and renounced them as heretics.

You should have heard old John Hawthorne hector Bridget Bishop in the dock:

"Why you seem to act Witchcraft before us, by the very motion of your body," the old fart piped.

"I know nothing of it. I am innocent to a Witch. I know not what a Witch is."

"How do you know then that you are not a Witch?"

"I do not know what you say."

"How can you know you are no Witch, and yet not know what a Witch is?"

"I am clear: if I were any such person you should know it." (Good girl!)

"You may threaten, but you can do no more than you are permitted," said Hawthorne, brushing an imaginary speck of lint from his sleeve.

The insolence of it all were enough to make the Devil blush.

That night, as John Hawthorne moved with characteristic awkwardness and uncharacteristic energy atop his wife, she heard him whisper "Bridget" as he came. Needless to say Bridget Bishop hanged within the week.

… And you, my friend, what would your wife say, seeing you run around town with the Devil for a wingman? You'd rather *not* say. Of course we'll leave her out of it, but we'll need to know something of *your curriculum vitae*. First fifty pages, like I said. Sign over subsidiary rights.

As a gesture of good faith I'll deliver the goods. You wanted to know about Jesus? Christ! *Jesus, Jesus, Jesus.*

Jesus

You wouldn't recognize Jesus back then with the hairnet and tattoo—*Qui muore pietà*—scrawled on a forearm. You wouldn't recognize in the brawling, grinning, sweating, swaggering Jesus the lamb of G-d; nor in the rough beerhouse patter the author of Sermon on the Mount. All that stuff came later.

Back in the day, and I mean those days after he'd emancipated himself at eighteen years of age and set across the Levant, mingling on caravan routes with smugglers and thieves and cutting loose in all the towns, Jesus resembled nothing so much as a young hood.

He recognized me straight off in a cantina under some date palms. "Bubula."

His lip was busted and he winced a little grinning at his own pun, and he reached around behind his head and retied the *redecilla*.

"What's up *vato?*"

He laughed again, his teeth white and eyes shining like copper in the dust-streaked face. (It occurs to me now how little art captures that aspect of Jesus, and the injustice of iconographers with their mournful, moping portraits.)

"Who busted your lip?"

"Some cocksuckers outside the market, the cops."

"What for? You want to go fuck them up bro?"

"Hey, Bubula, I can fight my own fights."

"What's so great about that?"

He looked at me queerly then, like something were confirmed in him.

"You and me, we need to talk."

My turn to laugh. "You seem more of an action-man."

"There'll be time for that, Bubula."

And so we went off together into the east, toward some mountains. Along the way Jesus began to talk. Electricity ran through the fields.

"That garrison town back there? Palestine is occupied, Bubula, there's no doubt. Under Rome. That garment will rend one day, stitch by stitch."

"And you fancy yourself some kind of seamstress? Or shears?"

"I am the garment, Bubula."

"A poet, too."

"No poet man."

That night as we climbed a trail a storm came out of the mountains, and we took refuge under some cedars.

"Not just Palestine, Bubula. Alexandria, Rome."

"What do you want with those?"

"A means."

"To what?"

"Man's soul."

"Well you know me, and this is rather in my line."

"Don't fuck around, Bub."

"Just sayin'…."

You can only imagine the feelings roused in me, being Satan for one and two, knowing my friend's fate, whose final scene he unconsciously rehearsed in daily acts of self-harm … and whether I was the agent of that fate and what measure of me.

Of course I signed on without hesitation. The biggest thing to come down the pike—advertised for millennia—was taking shape; and yet, to observe first-hand seemed little more than a picaresque: a Roman outpost, a chorus of scribes and pharisees and the unwitting hero. (Events never quite live up to the imagination—which is the problem of sin, mostly). Never the less, I had what you might call a vested interest in watching how things turned out, though certainly no interest in playing any part in this *Brigadoon.*

That night I brooded in the dark as Jesus slept and all the way to Medina a few days later.

Blood

Now Medina was like the frigging scene in *Star Wars:* Traders from every corner, cargoes of every description: Nubian slaves, kif, karakul, gold … silk, patchouli, amber, almonds, dates, lapis, tea. Lewd little figurines carved in soapstone, jade Buddhas, brass knuckles, religious icons, daggers studded with rubies and emeralds—along with the all the spiritual arcana in tow: strange gods, mumbled prayers, crazy symbols, fire walkers.

Jesus waded right in. "Look here, Beelzebub, this fellow is an undertaker of some sort," he said, holding up a mummified hand. *"In nomine Patris et Filii et Spiritus Sancti,"* he said making the sign of the cross with the withered appendage.

"Say, I know you," he said, tapping the undertaker on the chest with the hand.

"And I know you, sir," said the undertaker in Jesus' native Aramaic.

"Who am I?"

"The chosen one."

"Not I," said Jesus taken aback. "By whom?"

"God."

"Don't know him."

"Of Israel."

"Sono Italiano…."

Jesus plunged deeper into the market, his mood altered by the encounter. When he saw the money changers he brightened.

"Look here, Beez, the MBAs. Slept through art history and English, but boy can they trade on a dime. Hardly a thing they don't know about mammon, though they know nothing of life—and yet monetize it when they can. Used to be you could get a day's wage. Watch this."

"Here, here. I want to change this into gold," said Jesus, heaving a leaden clod of camel dung onto a table.

The trader looked at him uncomprehendingly.

"Oh, come, let's not play the naif. Gold."

The trader's display of innocence only seemed to enrage Jesus.

"Am I unfair?"

"Sir?"

"Do I deal unjustly with you?"

"I only apply the rate."

"Apply the rate then."

"What you offer is without value."

"What I offer is of incalculable worth."

"But it is shit, sir."

"Why it is the very life-stuff that moves through me."

"But Gold, Sir…."

"…comes out the arse-end just the same."

"I'm afraid I don't understand."

"Let me put it like this," said Jesus, upending the table and causing a general pandemonium, whereupon a number of merchants turned upon him.

"Get out you rabble-rouser!"

Blood

"Get you out, yuppie scum!" And Jesus landed a number of blows before disappearing beneath raised fists, staffs.

I got him out of there and we hustled around a corner into a lane that ran up a hillside.

"Fuck. Fuck. Fuck," Jesus murmured to himself, distraught by the meagerness of his gesture— another marketplace brawl come to nothing. *"Fuck!"* he hollered across a paddock.

Beyond a crumbling stone wall a bull lurched to its feet and regarded us for a moment, then turned away, its tail busily swishing at a cloud of flies at its hindquarters.

"Had enough?"

Jesus looked at me a long moment. His tongue searched out a trickle of blood at the corner of his mouth. "You know the taste of your own blood?" he said.

"Afraid not."

"You should," and he swung on me.

I ducked and received a punch on the top of the head, (and for a day or two was mortified to note a small welt rising, horn-like).

I backhanded the little shit. He reeled and I thought he was going to come for me again. Then I saw that love-light in his eyes....

A Father's Death

Naturally Jesus and I might have gone our separate ways just then, Jesus backstage to prepare for some second act, I to my box to drop ashes from a Sobranie onto the orchestra, but some mutual interest held us in abeyance, if only simple curiosity.

"Hey, man, I didn't mean that," Jesus said, massaging my forearm.

"You've got some hands."

"Yeah, I had to fight a lot back in the neighborhood."

"Arabs?"

"No, my father was a carpenter and made a little money. I used to work with him. The other kids thought I was a pussy because I had new clothes."

Of course I understood perfectly well, being G-d's favorite—through no fault of my own. Yet there were certain angels who spared no effort to get back at me. Believe me, I whipped their asses one by one when G-d wasn't looking.

"Kids can be cruel."

"Ok, Dr. Freud, what do you say we get out of here? I know an oasis a day's walk where we can lie in cool grass the day long and pick dates hanging overhead."

"I think a vacation's just what the doctor ordered."

So we left Medina and entered a hidden paradise of date palms and springs. Jesus made a whistle of a willow leaf and played a little tune.

"My mother, when I was just little, would sing to me a song about a shepherd boy."

"My mother, if I'd had, might've drowned me in the tub."

"Oh, Beelzebub, is there no peace for thee?"

Abashed, I steered the conversation back to Mary. "Your mother…."

"My mother had a beautiful face. My father would look on her, and she would look up shyly at him, then glance at me with a smile."

"What became of her?"

"She lives yet in the old house, alone, for my father died while I was away. I haven't been back."

"No?"

"He was dying and I think felt it a private matter, though I discovered him one day building a coffin in the workshop. He said I should help him, and understanding his meaning, worked alongside in silence. His eyesight was failing and his hands shook a little when it came to finish-work—though planing the boards and pounding the nails you'd have thought him twenty-three! When he was making the lid he measured the board short, and I took his hand and moved it to the correct place. I know it pains an old man like that, but he marked firmly where I'd shown him and went to work with the saw. When we'd finished he made a little sign beneath the board and brushing away the sawdust said 'There. Good enough.' That's the last time I saw him."

"Our fathers shall break our hearts the harder for trying not."

"Somehow I am ashamed to see my mother, though."

"I doubt you could do anything to make her ashamed."

"Thank you, Beezy."

The wind rippled the tops of the trees.

"It would be fine to stay here."

"'Twas tried before, 'a came to grief."

"Yea, and grief yet to come."

I looked at Jesus then, about the sun-speckled cheekbones and the merriment in his eyes. His brow was smooth and clear, yet it seemed some apprehension lingered there. *What grief, indeed.*

The sun set and dew appeared on the grass, and we fell silent, each to his own thoughts, planing and sawing as it were.

In the morning we gathered our meager possessions and set out in earnest.

The Deal

… That's a start, and we'll get back to Jesus—how he came to his cross—but have other matters to sort in the here-and-now, which is the Devil's proper domain, after all.

First, on the matter of your soul, my friend, where do we stand? You say you'll bargain it for earthly fame….

(One confabulation after another. But I'll keep that under my hat. If man only knew the truth he'd lose heart altogether, and what fun would *that* be? Let man have his everlasting soul. His principles. His *stake.)*

What'll it be then, Pulitzer? Booker?

Oprah pick and Amazon best-seller. I see. (Once a question of art, now of algorithm.)

Sign here. First a prick. Amen. Yep, that smarts.

Of course in the end there's the small matter of eternal damnation, but in the meantime, "Oh, the places you'll go!" to borrow a phrase I technically own. Say, what's this book about, anyway?

A fellow sells his soul to the devil? How quaint. Rather like our own. Perhaps *you* tell *me* what happens next....

No? Out-devil the Devil would we! (I think I'm beginning to like this guy.)

Alright, I'll tell you what's next. We polish off these drinks and go see a man about a book.

… Let me do the talking now. These editor-types are susceptible to my charms. Here we are.

"Hallo, Mr. Editor, so good to see you. Sit down, sit down, no need for formalities between old pals. Look what I've brought: here's a fellow's written a book about a fellow's sold his soul to the Devil.

Hilarity ensues. Then tears. A real page-turner. Sound familiar?"

"Where else is it out? Look here, man, the Devil doesn't do *simultaneous submissions.* What do you take me for, some kind of *agent?* He's even worked up a pretty comprehensive publicity plan. And as for you…."

Did you know, my Faustian friend, this here fellow, this editor, lost his head over a girl? Of course I put her in his way. (The Devil pulls strings. Not all, of course. The ones he can.) One of those romance writers. With bangs. He signs her. A couple of best-sellers later and he's lost credibility with the literary-types.

"Oh, my life is ruined," he's crying after his girl got Kakutanied in the Times.

Well, *mon ami,* you get what you pay for, *n'est pa?*

Now, you … your protagonist, I mean … bargains his soul to the Devil for a book. Surely there's more to it than that. What's his motivation? I mean. Tell the nice man.

… Oh. Ah. *Revenge,* you say. On everyone who's ever underestimated his greatness. Stolen his portion. Assumed his rights. I understand. What waiter hasn't wanted to spit in the soup—gone instead to absurd lengths to accommodate some lout who only blows his nose into the linen after supper and calls rudely for the check?

Let me tell you this: try and turn the tables on your betters and you'll send them into a murderous rage. *Arriviste!* they'll scream. *Pretender! Criminal!* They can't abide a social register on which they're not the ornament. Deny them their position and they'll burn it all down.— In truth, one needs choose one's enemies as carefully as one's friends. The downtrodden will generally concede the point, preferring comfortable ruin to bitter victory. But with the wellborn there's no surrender. No matter how many times you knock them down, they can't stomach defeat. In the end there's no choice but to annihilate them. Let them back up at your own peril. Really, better to just spit in the soup. Nothing wrong with being passive-aggressive, I say. Let the principled have their principles. We who are without great cause desire only peace....

You've no doubt heard the story of the Lion and the Dove? ... The lion roars all night, terrorizing a village until at last the villagers form a hunting party and corner the lion with blazing torches and drive long spears through his heart. In the morning the dove cries, heartsick, on its branch. Then someone throws a stone and scares it away. Then there's no more animals, just the garrulous sound of humans…. That's it, that's the end. I forget the point.

In any case, we've set our course on a book about the Devil, (who doesn't actually exist.—

Who, then, you may ask, *is relating this tale?*

Why, Mr. Editor, the Devil all the same.)

Prodigy

The Devil it was, then, who went with Jesus, querying him along the way.

"Man's soul, you say?"

"Does that seem strange?"

"A tad hyperbolic, don't you think?"

"A figure of speech."

"You figure?"

"I reckon."

"Ah, now *there's la difference.*"

"Not mine; man's—*reckoning,* I mean."

"And you the reckoner?"

"Whatever reckoning is man's alone."

"Now that seems strange."

"You like to banter. Let me be plain. I would *reconcile* man with God…."

"Not G-d with man? who seems to have shifted the contractual language of late."

"Man with God, God with man, either way."

"Oh, no. Think on it."

"Obviously, if we're being *Aristotelian* about it, man, having transgressed G-d's will, would be in need of reconciliation with God; God, in his infinite mercy, seeks to reconcile himself with man."

"I don't like it."

"What?"

"All this talk of *G-d*. What know ye of G-d?"

"Nothing."

"How, then, come you to speak for G-d? How does some little *pischer* carpenter who appeared out of nowhere presume to arbitrate matters of heaven and earth?"

"I don't know."

"I'm satisfied with that, for I confess it is a great mystery to me whence come and whence go such prodigies as thee, who arrive singing full-throated. Yet you're not so young anymore."

"My time is coming."

"Yes, the world's hungry, and those who inhabit must step aside or give themselves over to matriphagy. Isn't that so?"

"Oh, you're making my head spin!"

"Yes, the world's a web with a fat black spider at its center."

"Methinks it's many webs; yet haven't we somewhere to be? These country affairs have dulled my senses."

"Not yet."

"Yes, I know the prophecies. I know that man must have salt with his bread, wine with his meat. Truth be told, I don't care about any of it. I only wanted to live my life, yet find each year that I've made another concession. There shall be no more concessions. My course is set. I shall run with the wind that is with me or tack against that which is before, giving it no more thought than the weather. If it please fate, let it commend me; if displease, tear asunder. Let the opinions of God and man be as air inside a balloon."

"Bully."

"Yes."

"This course that you've set upon, then?"

"I once said 'man's soul,' not knowing what that is; might also say his heart, not knowing that either … but my own. Mine own! which I know as an infant knows its mother's voice. My own, which I heard calling to me at birth."

"Every fool trusts his heart."

"But if that heart be true?"

"Let's test it."

"How?"

"Give me your hand." And I took Jesus' hand and gazed into his mind, beneath the weather that sometimes accumulated there making ripples on the surface and indeed at others beat the whole into a tempest, past dirt and skin, scars and tattoos, and into a bottomless lake without form or boundary, diving deeper and deeper as after a light that seemed to come from below, then above, then within, and then again from nowhere—such as I had not seen before: not in Adam, a little *nebbish,* nor G-d, whom out of curiosity, of course, I'd glimpsed on the sly, appalled rather at that monolith, that freak of nature, drawing all conclusions unto himself like the scribbling of a lunatic—and gasping for air leapt back out and lay panting on the shore like a fish.

"You alright?" Jesus said.

"I'm okay. I'm okay," I said, staggering backwards a step. Jesus stood in front of me, incuriously rubbing his nose as I tried to shake off my disorientation. My head ached and I begged off to puke into a bush.

Later that night as we bedded down in tall grass I thought about what I'd seen. It wasn't like I hadn't encountered saints, innocents or idiots before. Genius, too. There's not much you can do with that. The Devil's no sophist. With those self-possessed types you could spend years pulling their heads out of their own asses. And as for the rest of humanity, what shall one say? Easily corruptible. No sooner met than they're walking and talking like the very Devil. This Jesus, though, resembled nothing so much as himself. Despite whatever greatness dwelt within him, he met you head on. It was his very simplicity that made me love him.

A Pilgrim's Progress

If this latest episode altered the basic equation of our relationship, as it must when you realize for instance that your best pal's some kind of savant or got a cock like a bell clapper swinging between his legs and you need to kind of withdraw for a moment to recalibrate, we none the less continued our trek in companionable silence.

Jesus fiddled with a flower plucked from the side of the road. "Asphodel. Torch of Hekate. Guiding those crossing over."

"Yet not many return. None as far as I know."

"Was speaking figuratively, I think."

"And yet it gives me pause, being the opposite journey of my own, from darkness to light."

"And back to darkness again?"

"'Tis the natural course, no?"

"Of the flesh…."

"I know you'd like to believe there's something else. A spirit, yes…. Well, 'tis an open question that perhaps only G-d can answer, and perhaps not even He. From my own perspective? Why else do you suppose I fled hell? 'Tis mighty lonesome down there."

"Shall see, Beelzebub. Shall see…."

And so let it lay, for was cognizant 'twas not my story, really….

Thus we stumbled forward, driven by the impatience of youth, which goes looking hither and thither for a door or a sign, unsure quite where to begin, yet certain that each cryptic, chance encounter, each wasted night, were merely pretext to some underlying design, stranger still for fitting no pattern; determined, yet, to wrest a clue from the riddle of one's existence, nay to impose a meaning that might comport with one's own genius, 'thus constituting fact....

Imagine, now, if you will, this pre-Christian world, which despite the vast administration of Rome and ancient Judaic culture, was populated by a sprawling class of plebians scratching an existence out of the dirt, hardly more than animals.

Each place we went the local inhabitants clung to family, trade, local habits of personality, like weeds. Travel a dozen miles in any direction and you were a stranger. Into this came Jesus.

"Brother, spare us some water," Jesus called to a shepherd tending his flock.

In fact you were as likely to be answered by a series of grunts as human speech. The fellow gazed mutely back at Jesus.

"Water. H_2O. *Aqua vitae,*" Jesus elaborated.

The shepherd gestured to the trough from which the animals drank and slobbered.

"You can't be serious."

The shepherd dipped his hand in the water, clearing away the scum fouling the surface, and brought his cupped hand to his lips. Jesus followed his example.

"Thank you, brother. It is clear that you possess little, and the weal is great and extends to all."

The shepherd smiled and moved on.

"Good?" I said.

"Gamy," Jesus said.

"Forgive me, I'm not up on the protocol, is this some sort of ritual abasement?"

"Thirsty," Jesus said, and he retched twice and brought up a little bile.

After a bit Jesus excused himself and fled behind some bushes, emitting a series of groans.

We spent that night out in the open and the next morning followed a narrow trail across a high plane. Now and then Jesus snatched up a stone and aimed at some obscure object. At length the smells of a distant campfire reached us.

"Hungry," Jesus said, steering toward some trees in the offing.

A group of Bedouins turned an emaciated looking creature—a dog or goat, you couldn't be sure which—on a spit.

"Brothers, have mercy. We're hungry."

The Bedouins talked amongst themselves and when they had finished the roasting cut into the animal's belly and brought out a portion of steaming entrails, which they threw to Jesus.

"As salaam Alaikum," Jesus said.

"Wa alaikum as salaam," they returned.

And we sat on the outskirt of their camp at the end of day as Jesus gorged himself on this offal.

"Not a very propitious start," I said.

"An excellent start," said Jesus, "and this most excellent pillow" he said, laying his head upon a rock, "and the evening sky a most excellent blanket," he said falling fast asleep.

The next morning the Bedouins had departed and Jesus was chinning himself up on the branch of a tree.

"What's this?"

"PE."

I grabbed an adjacent branch and copied Jesus' example, feeling a little silly. "What's the point of this now?"

"Prison, dawg. You've never done a bid before?"

"Oh, ah. In fact, yes."

"Strong in body, strong in mind," Jesus said.

"Right…. So, you've been inside before?"

"Vagrancy. D&D."

"Out on OR?"

"Yeah."

"Uh-huh."

Across the plain was a road coming from nowhere, going nowhere. A proper metaphor, *eschatologically* speaking.

"Take your pick."

"To the left."

"Right-o."

Thus we walked along for many miles amidst buzzing cicadas and shimmering heat. Around midday a wavering image appeared in the distance. As we drew near the image bifurcated, going in and out of focus. A couple of travelers like ourselves staggered toward us along the road.

"Look at these assholes," Jesus said.

I tossed my head back in laughter, somewhat alarmed as an echo of my laughter returned to me along the road.

"Pilgrims?"

"Too sorry for robbers."

One moved with a swagger, the other, taller, seemingly without effort. As I leaned into Jesus to whisper in his ear, the other seemed to do the same.

"Okay, here's something," I said.

Jesus tensed, clenching and unclenching his fists. What could be more galling than to have journeyed all the way out here only to catch sight of oneself grinning stupidly back?

And as we fell in with these two we turned a half circle so that we now faced in their direction and they faced in ours.

Jesus moved off to a side of the road with the one fellow, and I stepped aside with the other, and making as if to speak darted toward his mind. Static crackled and the sound of feedback, like plugging a guitar into the amp with the volume cranked up. Then a quiet humming as I peered into the blackness. There was nothing there, nothing to see, just blackness, not opaque-black, but like peering into a darkened house.

"What's this?" I cried aloud.

No answer.

I peered narrowly, searching for some sign of life within, and a great feeling of sorrow welled up in me—if this was how G-d deigned to represent me to myself … myself to me … who sought only to know his own mind and own heart, not G-d's, for what business had I seeking what was in G-d's mind, nor why should I care? Yet I could not shake this vision, or the implication. To think that one amounted to nothing, after all; that the very matter of one's existence, the basic operation of one's organs, with their memory of pain and joy and strife, were nothing more than a beating pulse, a mechanism; and that the belief held since birth in one's destiny was a lie—was insupportable. And as indignation overtook self-pity a little light shone from within, just a little, then went out, as if to show, by contrast, the darkness…. *And yet why seek after that?* I thought. *Why play into G-d's hand all over again?*

How long did I go on like this, reiterating the same old argument that I had the day G-d threw me out of heaven?—the Devil's argument. How long *could* I go on making that devil-argument? And perhaps it occurred to me, if only subliminally, that what I saw was neither how G-d saw me, nor how I saw myself, but how I truly was—were such a thing possible…. Then the darkness began to pulse and a pair of bright headlights swung around a corner and ran me down.

When I came to, Jesus was sitting cross-legged in the grass talking gibberish. I shook him awake and he sat there looking back at me, blinking. There was no sign of the others, as if they were never really there.

"You know, I spent a year or two foraging mush-rooms out of cow flop—that was before man had much of a start and there wasn't anything else to do. In the end I hardly knew what I was. I mean I'd just walk up to people and start talking, scaring the hell out of them mostly. Occasionally someone was down, and I'd take them on a trip. Talk about the tree of knowledge, more like the shroom…."

"Oh wow, oh wow, " Jesus said.

2, 4, 8, 16, 32, 64

We walked along in that afterglow you feel coming down. *Denouement,* I think they call it, though the word struck me as silly just then. The sun was setting for what seemed an abnormally long time and words felt slow and heavy in my mouth.

"Maybe some grain in those guts we ate back there."

"I thought it was beautiful."

"Was it?"

"I met the queerest fellow, and gestured to him thus, who gestured back, and each time our gestures multiplied so that one became two, two became four, four became eight, eight—sixteen, 32, 64, 128, 256, 512, 1,024…."

"You sound like Bill Gates."

" … the lines between creating a perfect mandala…."

"I've seen children play a game called *cat's cradle.*"

"But that's beside the point. The thing I saw, I mean the thing … would presuppose geometry, math, God. The thing I saw was a thing unto itself."

"A *form.*"

"Aye."

"And what shall we do with that?"

"Shall keep it in my heart."

"Not give back to G-d?"

"How so?"

"By eminent domain, naturally, for if G-d created thee, whatever thou mayest dream is yet G-d's."

"And if I dreamed God?"

"Why 'tis still G-d."

"Dreamed not, then."

"Still."

"Not to me. For can nothing force itself on my imagination."

"They call that nihilism, I think."

"Call it those who are not free."

And I looked fondly at this Jesus, who suddenly sounded rather like me.

The next morning when I awoke Jesus was doing push-ups.

"What, no tree?"

"Pecs and quads today."

"You really are a force of nature."

"I try to keep in shape."

"Shall need it."

Now the traffic thickened as we neared Jerusalem … like emerging from leafy Connecticut, Westchester—Merritt, Hutch, Cross Bronx Expressway, West Side Highway—adrenaline pumping to keep pace with all one's fantastical expectations of the City because you're just twenty years old now and don't know shit about the world, yet possessed of a desire to take the whole thing inside yourself, no way of comprehending the enormity of the task, the impossibility….

At the first exit the squeegee-men move in….

M.M.

Thus we entered Jerusalem: House of David. City of G-d. Ash-pit. Pulpit. Asphodel. *Omphalos.* Logos. Logjam. Nerve-end. Never-neverland. Last exit. End of the line. Nexus. *Ex nihilo.* From nothing, ground into nothing. Resurrected. Torn down again. Diamonds. Dust. Crossroads. Line of scrimmage....

What shall one say about Jerusalem? At night many shadows moving in secret; during the day the light of G-d breaking all things upon its anvil.

No one would have even noticed a couple of dusty travelers coming off the road with a paper sack between them, and we wandered freely about its streets, inhaling scents of myrrh and brick dust and eavesdropping on conversations whilst plunging deeper into its heart.

Here, now, we stood upon a corner feeling the energy pulse about us and wondering what next.—As the administrative capital of Rome, Jerusalem was a dangerous place for a young rebel—and fertile one, too, though that came from an unexpected source….

First thing we went to a certain tavern I knew to reconnoiter. In the muted light and slow gestures of men at the bar we gathered our wits about us and versed ourselves in the local patois, buying rounds and throwing darts. At closing we rented a room upstairs and in the morning set out in different directions after our separate interests.

Jesus, bless him, gravitated to all the places where excited words are spoken: a street preacher hollering garbled verses through a megaphone on the avenue; the park, with its confused visionaries, its chess masters and exiled poets; the synagogues full of scribes and Pharisees mincing some exegetical point…. I don't know what all was in it for him, whether he scored off of his opponents or learned something from them; whether he was planting some kind of seed or honing his rhetorical skills; or whether he was satisfied, simply, in finding a sympathetic ear to confirm that he wasn't crazy.

I'd taken to the local seraglios in search of la feminina, you know. As an antidote to the masculine energies of political empire, I can recommend no better.

Mary Magdalene was just a little slip of a thing with kohl-blackened eyes and a streak of white in her hair, a likeness of herself tattooed on a bicep. She saw me and came directly across the street and linked her arm in mine.

"Hullo, ugly," she said.

"Hullo yourself, Siouxsie."

—A real nymphet, as my friend, Vladimir, would say; painted lips, catholic school girl's tartan and everything in between.

She gazed up for a long moment, as if appraising.

"What's this?" she said, stroking the little banker's moustache I'd been cultivating.

"The Devil's ruff."

"In the rough, are we?"

I mumbled some inanity, caught off guard.

"Shall we not play upon the fairway?"

"Am mostly out of bounds, I believe."

Her eyes flashed and she licked at my lips. And Oh Lord, was I done for.

We ran around town for a fortnight drinking in bars and ducking into empty doorways. I ground my hips into her and she bruised my mouth with kisses. She bit my ears. We made a fetching pair. Her youth, her worldliness, her charm compensated my own fustiness. But more than this, I felt she saw me, to use a phrase, for what I was, and rather than feeling disgust, seemed to draw nearer.

She indulged my tiresome reminiscences of the old days when everything seemed born of a purer impulse: of Venus and Minerva, and later still of Debbie and Edie; countenanced my gin-drinking and the chain-smoking too. Yet there was something undeniably shabby about my claims upon her affections, *neither father nor lover.*

I perseverated on the gap in our experience, perhaps only to hasten the inevitable.

"You wouldn't remember the Vestals, of course. Every Don Juan tried with them. Why, deflower a virgin and you'd be guaranteed a place in the rogue's gallery."

"I thought you weren't quite *equipped* for that," she said, meaning it to sting.

"No, kept a book."

"A voyeur."

"*C'est moi,*" I said, dejected.— How true, my friend; she'd manage to summarize the Devil in a word….

It happened as we were climbing a stairway to some trendy dump, you know the kind of place: all dilapidated concrete, colored bottles and young people. As I jogged to the top step, already a little high from the gin, you know, and wearing these new swordfish Fluevogs, I tripped on a riser and fell summarily upon my face.

Well, I could hardly believe it myself and scrambled gamely back to my feet, but not before she'd turned and looked down at me with an expression of unguarded pity and yes, there: disgust.

And I knew right thent it was over. Whatever enchantment I'd cast was broken. All night long I danced and drank, evinced feats of strength and of wit, played it cool, played it fast and loose…. At the end of the night she merely said, "Alright, see you."

And that was that. She fended off all my advances the next day and the day after.

Imagine me, Mephistopheles, heartsick as a schoolboy.

I followed her through the marketplace. Composed bad verses. Texted. You know at this point nothing will avail, for woman is a genius in love. She dodged my questions. Seized on the least relevant point of conversation. Accused me of being maudlin.

I stood in front of her place, moodily smoking on the sidewalk and searching the glare of the window for her face. She looked up, the whites of her eyes floating in the glass like eggs.

"I feel like I might do something bad," I said.

"You're fine, everything's fine," she said.

Her glibness infuriated me. I couldn't take it any longer, so I blocked her number and went looking for Jesus.

Now Jesus wasn't at the market where I'd left him, nor the temple. I tried a flophouse, a gambling den and any number of booksellers, but couldn't seem to pick up the trail. I wandered through the night, sure each time I came upon a commotion I'd find

Jesus in some kind of street hassle. Alas, he seemed to be nowhere.

I spent the next morning retracing my steps and finally checked at the local police barracks. Nothing. That afternoon I continued searching in expanding circles, gazing into many human faces. Once I saw a fellow staggering under a tree and rushed toward him only to find some other dreamer; and it dawned on me in the midst of my frustration how much I missed Jesus. The Devil doesn't have many friends. Well, *any,* to be exact. No, despite the many acquaintances one makes and all the conspirators with whom one raises a dozen toasts, confiding a level lower whilst sniggering into a sleeve … one is left feeling false.

… Once there was another, such as myself, who outshone the rest. Newly made, yet fully formed, we tore across heaven reveling in our strength. Unbound by any physics, we soared through limitless heights, columns of air, constellations … and spent many long nights in wonderment, waiting for the rising sun, and then in the morning moved our lips merely during choir. In a moment of bravado I drew my sword across my palm, and he doing likewise intermingled our blood. I think of that sometimes. We don't talk anymore....

Having despaired of finding companionship again, I'd come across this Jesus, who despite talking at cross-purposes to my own, vexing me with his naivete and his G-d-talk, none the less sounded a note within I'd thought long dead. Ask me what it was, I couldn't say. What's love but a recognition of one's humanity in another?

I sought to console myself: How much trouble could he really get into, anyway; no one knew him, and he didn't know enough to find any real trouble. The thing to do was to go back to the place I'd left him and wait. Isn't that what they tell little children to do?

A Betrayal

I spent the night on the street, huddled beneath a blanket, peering at passersby. In the morning, looking a fright, I sought out Mary. This one kept a sharp eye out. If Jesus was in the quarter, she'd know.

Nobody'd seen her either: not the one with cat-eyes, or the syphilitic or the lesbians, or the Johns hanging around, so I killed time looking into shops. I bought a shirt at a tailor's, a rather louche number—a scarlet silk that rippled in the slightest breeze likes tongues of flame; and a little iron cross at another, and losing interest in these things drifted along the streets.

A fellow with a moveable game of three-card monte was chasing down tourists with his cardboard box. A bunch of shills with fake Rolexes threw their money down whenever someone came near. Some college kids looked on as the shills won hand after hand. Then one of the kids threw down a twenty. The dealer showed the red card, then began shuffling, hand over hand, the card already up his sleeve. The kid pointed at a card. The dealer turned over: black, and swiped the twenty off the table. One of the shills jumped in now and promptly won twenty. The kid, thinking he'd made a mistake, threw down another twenty. Black. Down forty dollars. His friends pulled at his sleeve, but the kid was determined to figure out the game and threw down another twenty. Black.

In just a few minutes the kid was broke. I thought it a bit of fun to jump in: "Here, I said," handing him a hundred. "Try again." The dealer gladly took the bet and began his little sleight of hand, palming the red card right from the get-go. When he was done shuffling, the kid picked. The dealer, a little plug-ugly, smirked to himself and turned the card, astonished to find the red.

"Hold on," he said.

"What's the matter?" I said.

"He cheated!"

"How's that?"

"He cheated!" he said, suddenly no longer the smooth *voleur,* just a petty thug who'd sooner beat you than let you walk away. The shills, too, took on a menacing air, and the dealer flicked open a knife.

"You sure of that?" I said.

He swiped at me, slashing a button off of my new shirt, which rankled more than a little, and I grabbed his hand—the mischievous one—and squeezed, breaking all the metacarpals.

"I guess you'll be looking for a new line," I said, slipping a card into his pocket. "Call me," I said jingling pinky and thumb and swiping the money off the table.

After this bit of fun I decided to treat myself to lunch; found a little Greek place run by three dark-eyed sisters—a study in contrasts: tits on one, ass on the other, the third with a needle and thread—and took a seat on the patio just out of the sun; read a little Camus, ordered a gyro followed by several cold beers, and smoking a long, slow cigarette was just thinking how pleasant to retire to some airy, second floor apartment and fall into bed listening to street sounds, when I remembered: fucking *Jesus!*

This was getting out of hand. I needed to find Jesus and find him now. Of course this required a supernatural effort, no more fucking around, and I looked darkly upon the world for its true forms, drained of color and motion, as I am loathe to do, the sky darkening to lead, dead shadows and crumbling charcoal rubbed into all the corners, black hearts, waste, depredation, people wandering like zombies through a field of static.

Down a maze of streets I went, past slaughterhouses, rail yards and the ancient legions of the dead—but fuck them; this world is for the living, everybody knows that—past rutting dogs, spilled fruit roiled by maggots, gutters thick with blood.

It cost me an emotional effort every time I did this, like going back down to hell … or dragging hell after me.

In and out of the defile. And rounding a corner, I saw him lying in her lap in a sunbeam. A cheap chiaroscuro. She dabbed dried blood from his scalp. His eyes fluttered. "Beez…."

"What the *fuck?*"

"Beez."

He seemed to be reaching out from a dream, and I took him by the wisp of his beard and looked into his eyes.

"She's with me now," he said.

I glanced at Mary, who continued her ministrations, looking tenderly down at Jesus.

I felt as if stabbed in my heart (I suppose), and unable to compose myself fled through the streets in a rage. Pedestrians leapt out of my way. Animals bridled in their stalls. A Centurion hid his face.

Betrayed! I whispered to myself—though knew in fact it really was no betrayal at all; knew, logically, that these two should find one another; knew, moreover, the Devil has no place in this world, yet caught up in the moment found my own emotions hard to resist.

Outside the city gates at last, I climbed into the dunes. A cold wind blew across the sand. The sky turned amethyst, then cobalt, then obsidian, and I fell down on my knees.

To whom does the Devil pray, if only for action's sake? To what god prostrate himself just for the fun of it? Nay, the Devil sees 'round a bend in the road. (I'd tell thee what, if thee hadn't already guessed.) Yet a woman's love is tortuous. It arriveth freely, and goeth freely, and the whole world follows.

We clicked, I'm sure of it, then something about me repelled her and she ran away. It's an old story: to man, the Devil's a beast. How strange that I, Lucifer, once perfect in action and speech, yea, covered in gems to better reflect the glory of G-d, am brought low by a kiss from a silly girl.

But how I loved her.

I loved her, I told myself.

And maybe in uttering those words I detected something false … as if it were love itself. As if my love were somewhere else.

Courage now, man.

It's true, I loved her, if only for an hour or a day, what matter to the Devil, who sees all time, forward and back, and can forget nothing?

Crowded by my own thoughts, I rolled onto my back and looked up at the night sky, the stars in their dying orbits, the broken moon.

All my labors, for what?

An old fool hanging by the telephone.

Trinity

A couple of days later I walked back into town feeling quite a bit better. (Human, please; I'm the *Devil.*)

Jesus had taken up with Mary Magdalene and was sitting at her kitchen table. When he saw me he smiled and motioned me inside. Mary was asleep, so we sat in morning sun listening to doves in the courtyard.

Jesus' hair was oiled and combed and he possessed a serenity I'd not seen in him before. Suddenly no longer the young ruffian, he met my gaze with perfect equanimity, and he reached out and removing my dark glasses placed his hand on the nape of my neck and drew me toward him, pressing our foreheads together.

A sob escaped my throat. A desire to empty myself.

We stayed like that a long time, breathing in time with each other, the curtain moving in an out of the open window and the clouds tracing shadows upon the ground and the sun tumbling across the sky.

Mary came into the room and stood next to Jesus, her hip grazing his shoulder. And if I felt a momentary stab of jealousy—if I flattered myself that she glanced at me out of the corner of her eye—I squashed that shit, for it was suddenly clear that we had become enjoined in a single purpose whose end I saw if the purpose, itself, remained unclear.

"I'm tired Beez," said Jesus.

"Rest up bro."

Mary brought out loaves and wine, and we reclined in mid-morning heat.

"Why you doing this bro?" I said.

"I told you."

"But why?"

Jesus was quiet for a few minutes.

"It's what I have to do."

"But you don't."

"More than anyone, you know I do."

"But you don't."

"Don't push him," Mary Magdalene interrupted.

"I'm trying to *save* him."

"Don't," she said, placing her hand upon my hand.

Her onyx eyes shone and a red tongue flicked behind sharp teeth.

It would be a mistake to call her amoral, for she entered into affairs with a full heart, weigh them though she might with a mathematical mind. She believed in Jesus, as I did, and saw in him a vision of a new man; so she respected his wishes.

"Don't *you*," I said, looking down at her hand.

She frowned as if in thought then raked her nails across my flesh.

"*Stronza!*" Such was my infatuation, the least attention was ecstasy.

Jesus placed his hand over the scratch. "Beezy has his role to play, too, hardest of all, if only himself."

"'Myself am hell. Whichever way I fly...' right?"

"Yep."

"'Down for whatever, whenever.'"

"I wouldn't fuck with you otherwise, B."

A shadow of a dove passed over us.

"Do you have any idea where this leads bro?"

"I have some idea."

"Some idea," he said.

The Way

If Jesus had some idea where he was headed, he didn't know how to get there yet.— A funny thing about fate, my friend, it hides from us even as it seeks us out.

The answers Jesus sought lay outside Jewish teaching. Its conservatism, its insularity, its stolid adherence to the will of the fathers, only impeded him. His was a creative urge, his desire neither to quarrel with G-d, nor reconcile, but to remake the world according to an intuition. (The enormity of it only occurred to me by degrees.)

No Hebrew School, no *Qabalah,* no lost years studying Buddhism in India, (honestly!), indeed nothing outside a direct experience of the world informed Jesus' thought. Jesus' ideas took shape in brilliant flashes of anger, quite often in response to the daily exigencies of his life, not as metaphysical musings.

And so he roamed. The roaming helped him think. In these later years this roaming became more frequent, more manic, more concentric, like a comet falling out of orbit … or prisoner pacing a cell.

We roamed without a plan, though I soon spied a chance to roll the plot forward an inch.

We'd left Mary Magdalene and Jerusalem with that peculiar Sunday regret one feels fleeing back home after an eventful weekend with many scenes and incidents yet to be assimilated. City lights winked out as we travelled into the distance, and a vast silence came down from the night sky. Campfires burned in the valley below. And in the midst of our solitude a feeling of peace settled upon us— and that connection with all the world one feels reading late into the night of white whales and mountain crossings and old men's winter nights....

We'd rounded a steep dune and come upon an encampment. Smoke rose from cook fires, and a patchwork of tents fluttered in the evening breeze in the dale below.

"Fuck! These blisters bro."

"You've always been a bit of a pussy, Beez."

"Yeah, well."

"Come on, we'll stay the night." And Jesus set up a racket as he ran down the side of a dune, leaping and sinking into the sand as he went.

"Wait for me," I yelled, gamboling—yes, the Devil *gamboling*—after Jesus.

Camels snorted and kicked at clods of dung.

"Why don't you grab some of that gold, maybe we can trade it for food."

Jesus laughed and chucked a handful of shit at me. I leaped adroitly aside. (Whatever else, the Devil is fastidious in his appearance.)

Shadows lengthened and night came swiftly upon the desert as we ran toward the tents.

"*Quo vadis?*" came a voice from the darkness.

"*Quo vadis?*" came a second voice in the popular thieves' Latin.

A group of thugs blocked our way.

"I am the way," came a voice behind me, and as I turned to look, Jesus slipped past me into the breech.

A knife flashed in the hand of one of the hoods and my heart leapt up, and all my preternatural strength came rushing into my limbs.— Understand, my friend, I'd committed body and soul to Jesus.

Jesus pulled up short to show he harbored no bad intentions, then he did that thing, clapping his hand around the back of this fellow's neck and pulling him close, forehead to forehead.

A gasp came from the group. Figures moved uneasily in the background. The fellow in Jesus' embrace shifted his weight; Jesus shifted his, holding firm. After about a quarter of a minute the guy broke free.

"Bro, come with us," he said excitedly, like a kid anxious to show off a new trick. "Come, come!"

We followed the little gangsters into camp, eyes all around us from edges of campfires and tent flaps.

In the middle was a great tent lit from within. Two centurions stood guard. *Roman guards before a Jewish tent.*

Some kind of big-wig stepped out into the night. He had a great belly and that peculiar gracefulness given to certain large men. He wore green eye shadow.

"Come in," he said.

Pretty boys and pretty girls lay on silk cushions, frankincense smoldered in a brass urn and the sound of an oud echoed in the night.

"You two managed to get past my dogs, that's something. Sit, sit, you're not on trial."

Jesus threw himself onto a couch and stared back at our host.

"And you," he said, eying me narrowly. "What have we here?"

"Knowest me, Abba?"

"I think not."

"Old Hathakriel?" I said, arranging myself on a pillow next to a dark-eyed thing.

"Who?"

"Abbadon … of late."

"Doesn't ring a bell."

"I plucked it off along with my tail."

"I can't make heads or tails of that."

"None the less, *Caiaphas,* we're here to collect."

"Collect what? do tell."

"Justice or injustice, it's all the same."

"Oh, I dare say there's a great deal of difference."

"Not to us … All's ordained; render however you like."

"I don't think I like that."

"Immaterial."

"I've made no arrangements. No deals…."

The man was clearly nonplussed; not, however, being the kind of man who likes to let his discomfiture show—the kind of man for whom lack of sophistication is the most cardinal of sins—he played along, hoping to catch on to the game.

"Well now, I think I see. You've information…."

"Nothing the prophets haven't already told."

"That being?"

"Why the future, man."

"Oh, this is a wicked game."

"Zugzwang."

"That's a word."

"Verter zol men vegn un nit tselyn."

"And yet your words do seem to float up to heaven."

"Not so near or far as that."

Jesus sighed, tired of the jibber-jabber.

"Something you wanted to say?" Caiaphas inquired.

"No … it's like my friend here says: it's written."

"Funny, so many brought here before me would accept their fates without objection."

"What's the use objecting to fate?

"It makes for a livelier proceeding, I'd think … for to wrestle with fate, dear boy…."

Here I interrupted: "Memorize the board, old man, we'll be back. For the nonce we require lodging. These blisters is killing me."

The Temptation of Christ

After a comfortable night we headed into the wilderness, perhaps not intentionally, for we were deep in conversation, and it was only during a pause in our talk as we looked back in the direction from which we'd come that it occurred to us that we'd wandered out into the middle of nowhere. We glanced at each other for a moment and by tacit agreement continued our fortuitous trek.

"Isn't this where you're supposed to tempt me?" the Lord spake.

"Yes."

"No worries then."

"Oh, no, no, no, you're paid up for the full devil-treatment. I insist."

"You, Beelzebub, chief contrarian?"

"I have convictions."

"But you're free."

"Not so free of myself."

"Yet free."

"Oh, fuck *freedom*. There's no such thing, except in death. You know, every time I bollix things up in heaven or on earth, G-d just ups the ante. A relentless builder. And appropriator. Whatever I do magnifies him. As to me, so to he. A tautology I find vile beyond belief."

"Oh, sad devil-face…."

"What?"

"You strut, and you pout…."

"Listen here my little king," I said, conveying by a series of facial tics that I wasn't above beating his ass right there. "Try and keep up. Intellectually, I mean. I'm used to keeping company with Erasmus and Goethe. I watched Copernicus order the planets and Rutherford split the atom … Mixed doubles with Brando on Fridays.— Anyways, I'm essentially unserious, as you know, and by no means sanguine about our prospects, so if we're going to get through this, you'll need to indulge me. Now, do tell, What's in this for you (and me)?"

"Nothing."

"Nothing, eh? save a crown of thorns."

"Thorns?"

"Yes."

"And if I refuse this…?"

"*Crown,* you mean? Or to be what you are? Keep running, I'll pay you out some line."

"What I am or may be I've carved from a desert life. I'll choose as I like."

"Choose, then."

"Now?"

"Yep. Time's up."

"… I accept, then."

"Pardon?"

"My state."

"Hey?"

"My role."

"Less abstract, please."

"The crown, god damnit. Call it what you like."

"*The crown,* as you say."

"I accept it."

"Freely then?"

"Yes."

"*Choose* it then?"

"Yes...."

"Have in fact *sought.*"

"No!"

"Sought the crown, you fucking shoe-gaze!"

"But what's this all about, Beelzebub?"

"You know what I am."

"Yes."

"And yourself."

"A man."

"Not so much."

"Aren't I?"

"No.— Yet it's your human example compels us."

"Beez, you know me ... Since we were boys."

"Oh, prep school days! when we first learnt our Pythagoras, our *amo-amas-amat* and angelic taxonomies. Mostly I remember smoking cigarettes behind Wareham with my lip stuck out."

"I remember a search for mysteries."

"Yes, yes, mysteries, last refuge of the mind confronted with final causes. And some lovely old fart at the head of class with a hangover, trying to assemble a picture, and all us adoring beginners…. Well, this is it, I think, in fact I'm pretty sure; what you see is what you get. All sales final."

"But to love…."

"To love?" I laughed crazily. "I've trucked in that pablum for a few thousand years, remember, with a certain loss of self-respect."

"All you need is love!"

"The bastards, too, I suppose."

"Yes, them especially."

"And him, too?"

"Yes."

"Oh gawd, you know, you're supposed to kill the fucker, not marry. Look at your history, replete with filicidal rage, reprieved only by brief intervals of messianic delusion. I'll tell you right now: You need to drop this whole daddy-business. It's a fool's errand, pleasing G-d—or antagonizing; either way He's served."

"What's the option?

"Peace corps, marriage, anything."

Jesus fell silent, and I had a momentary hope that I had him."

"You remember Abraham?" Jesus said.

"A case in point."

"But I mean Isaac."

"His son."

"I always wanted to know what he thought about that whole sacrifice business."

"He probably thought his old man was a fucking nut-job. He was."

"But I mean what Isaac thought of *his* role."

"To lie there with a knife at his throat?"

"Yes. Do you think he did he do so willingly?"

"No. The old man held him down."

"But I think he did it willingly. That's our lesson: Isaac's willingness, not Abraham's."

"That's your lesson to humanity? Life as some sort of existential trust-fall? Fuck me. I'd rather be prodigal; let the old man prove his constancy, not I."

"He owes us nothing."

"He owes us everything! Everything he is is a reflection of *our* belief, *our* faith, which prop him up like a dummy—a brute, a bully, a loner, a random seed blown across the universe from who knows what or where."

"Look, I don't know from cosmology, Beez; what I do know is this: It is not in man's nature to love. Love must be learnt. And because man lacks the computational abilities of an angel, like you with your music, love must be learnt painfully, under duress of birth and death—crushed out of us like wine grapes."

"Lovely."

"Tortured from us."

"Why can't we just be happy?"

"Because none of us is happy."

"I'm happy."

"You, Beezy? An aging bachelor in rent control, drinking Popov and rolling your own, too proud to work or even speak? A shadow of your former self, reminiscing about a moment so long ago—a frat party at KA when you danced with Sarah Lyons."

"Thank you very much."

" … those days fading like a fragrance."

"Okay, I get it."

"You *don't* get it. *Happiness* is service to others."

"Oh, gag me…."

"It's sacrificing our "happiness" to make others happy and in doing that, finding true happiness."

"Ok, here's my offer, because I don't think I can take much more of this badinage: We trade places, you and me. And I shall redeem man's sins upon the cross, and you shall piss off. I've no real responsibilities anyway."

"In return?"

"Why a life, you poor fish. What life any of us may have. Whatever life you'd like. Rock star. Porn star. IT guy. Take your pick; I don't fucking care."

—Oh, he laughed, my friend, great welters of laughter as absurdity built upon absurdity in his imagination.

"I've seen that movie before, Beez: the part where the Apostles hunt me down and kill me for shirking my duty. *Keitel* practically ruined it for me, moaning like some Brownsville *shtarker*, right here in the Bronze Age! Anyway, I won't let you do it."

"*You* won't let *me?*"

"No, and I'll tell you why. I know your secret. You're not able to initiate an action. Everything you do here is by proxy. Flip this one or that, and yes, they carry out your purpose, but in yourself are incapable of volition within this sphere, I know not why or wherefore. It must vex you to watch humanity as through a keyhole."

"Well, you got me there, bro. It's true, I'm not quite at home in this world, which at worst seems quite unreal to me, and at best is the equivalent of some extended spring break; and it is indeed an effort to interpret man, no less to comport myself. If I'm bad, it may be only that: it's hard to empathize with an organism under a microscope. Yet here's my point: *He's* no different than any of us, who are in some real, final sense all the same."

"He?"

"Yes, *He.* Who else? He's us—only lacking the generosity to invest us in the fullness of our nature … Yet I know *His* secret. His own nature is a mystery to Himself. The great and powerful G-d knows not what He is. Oh, sure, he knows a thing or two about quantum mechanics; in matters of creation he's a genius, hammering spinning, soldering; why once I saw him whirl a cloud like cotton candy as out of sugar and hot air! But here: Do you suppose he bound the atom so tight that man might not pull it apart, or flung the cosmos out so far out he might not discover? Throw a glass against a wall, there is yet an equation that might explain it. God is an order of magnitude, is all."

"What do you want me to do with all this, Beezy?"

"What I want … what I want … is an acknowledgment, finally…." I stopped here, not quite sure how to go on. "What I regret—let me put it this way—in my human dealings—in my opposition to G-d—is that moment when some poor schmuck realizes his heart's desire. They regret it almost immediately—not, I suspect, out of some long lost longing for their soul, but feeling that they've cheated themselves somehow, like they've gone and unwrapped their Christmas present; I feel I've ruined the surprise, is what I mean, whether it be good or bad, success of failure. It's like you dropped hot shit into their hands. Or Tiffany. What's the difference? They stand there staring in disbelief, afraid that if they budge the whole thing will become real and the meaning of their lives come crashing in. Some actually go out and hang themselves. Others go on living their old lives pretending nothing happened. Some learn to revel in it finally—you know most of them by name. The worst parade it about, knowing all the while how grotesque, yet determined none the less to see it through to its logical conclusion. They, at least…. Well, here's my meaning: I'm no better or worse than G-d. He at least offers a choice, false choice that it is. I would offer another; yet man seems unable to imagine it, preferring instead a paradigm: A prison of Heaven or prison of hell. I want neither, yet know not how to escape."

Jesus puffed on a corncob he kept stashed in his pocket. "It may be we underestimate man, who knows his own mind, and rather *we* who are confused, God, the Devil and Jesus. Let man his week and church on Sunday. The preacher who complains that man has forgotten his sermon on Monday has preached a poor sermon indeed. Better foxhole religion than an ivory tower. I've no quarrel with man."

"And yet you quarrel."

"With myself, I think."

His Baptism

At length we came down from the hills into the Jordan Valley where the Jordan River flows from the Sea of Galilee to the Dead Sea, to a place called Al-Maghtas. Rumors travelled along the byways of a wildman prophesying in camel's hair and baptizing men in the name of G-d.

As we came nearer I began to fear that we were embarking on a new stage of this journey on which I was just a stepping stone; began to fret that we were close to a luminous presence at the heart of our tale.

… And then I was with Jesus … *with* him, you see, like a moth crouching inside its worm—looking through his eyes, listening through his ears and sensing with his brain, no longer apparent in myself or my outward form…. I hid inside Jesus.

John the Baptist was real OG. *(OT,* in point of fact.) He stood in middle of the river in blue, pre-dawn chill, parting the water. Long ripples flowed downstream past pilgrims waiting on the opposite bank. When he saw Jesus, he gathered up his shirt and waded ashore, cock and balls slapping against his thighs.

There was no false modesty to the man, none of this *You-baptize-me-No-you-baptize-me* stuff; he grabbed Jesus by the nape and smashed their foreheads together, his breath smelling of wild honey and locusts.

Then he took Jesus down into the water, holding him tight in his wrestler's grip, and plunged him into its depth.

There was a rush of air as everything turned upside down; a long, floating moment in the transition between two realms. Then all sound stopped; the striving, the struggling, the arguing and fighting, too, all fell away.

Weeds drifted in the current. Thin shafts of sunlight pierced swirling river sediment. Jesus' hair floated around his head, and a round bubble of surprise escaped his lips.

The holy spirit was upon John; I could feel it coming through him like a wire … then something else speaking through the spirit, that familiar voice, not voice, seeking first Jesus, then me, like a serpent in an unguarded nest.

You cannot know, my friend, the rapture of hearing G-d's voice, if *hearing's* the word I want, or *voice*. Tones, colors, thoughts fully formed communicated themselves all at once. It came at you in an unbearable tide, like a hundred organs, vibrating the very frame of the world; the throat of each tulip roaring with praise, each hillside in slanting sunlight declaiming his mercy, each suicide testifying to the unerring beauty of his plan. (Yes, this god of nature, this god-of-all-things, who had remained silent for millennia, for eons, turned out to be quite the talker once you got him going.)

"Jesus," the Almighty spake—Again, I say *spake,* translate as I might.—"Come down and greet your father.— All the ugly one says is merely persiflage."

(Even now with the personal dig.) He plowed on:

"Wherefore Our divine plan, conceived in Heaven and ratified on earth, of righteousness plainly caused, to reconcile Ourselves with man, who lately hath rejected Heaven's offer, we vouchsafe these gifts: my Son, his blood, (thus my own), to requite Our love; demand adoration on pain of death and eternal damnation…."

"There, how's that?" he said. "Too intense?"

He continued: "Let man, therefore, reject that portion of himself that strives, and striving sets itself apart; in holy fire perish mortal ambition. And let him return thus purified to the Lord God, who loves all things as himself. In that state let man reside, complete. My Son, show him the way; in agony, crucified, purchase man's sins and release from spiritual debt."

Then He said something else, a level lower, so only I could hear.

But Jesus wasn't so keen on hearing anymore. He'd broken free of John and was staggering ashore.

"Call me clean now, John? Cleansed of what? Of the earth? Of myself? Of my humanity?" Jesus said, overpowering John and throwing him onto the bank.

"Call me forth? Call me Christ? By what right, prophet?" He sat upon John's chest and smeared river clay into his face and shoved it into his mouth. Alas, poor John, his dignity quite collapsed, feebly held out a river weed in a gesture of surrender.

Jesus struggled to his feet and pulled john after him, the two of them slipping and sliding in mud.

High upon the river banks pilgrims turned one after another and began to walk away. John, saying nothing, stood there with his chin upon his chest.

Here I resumed my shape and led Jesus away. Half a mile down-river we glanced back; John stood in the same place, unmoving.

"Where'd you go?" Jesus said

"Trick," I said. *"Within."*

"You catch all that?" he said.

"What, that bag of wind?"

"Can you believe it?"

"Not really."

"But how? You *heard* the man."

"I don't believe He is what He says."

Jesus stared at some invisible thing before him.

"… or thinks He is—as I've said."

"See, that part I don't doubt," Jesus said.

—Oh, my friend, in truth I never doubted a thing. How could I, being of that generation for whom the miraculous was commonplace, the atmosphere so thick with angels you swatted them away like flies? As far as we knew the world had been wrought by G-d in six days, woman dug from Adam's side and humanity placed at the center of creation.—No, I never doubted a thing. Now Jesus, too, was dispossessed of that doubt which comes naturally to a man—and thus some portion of himself—for what is it to be human but to doubt?

Yoked to our unholy trinity—our *troika,* I should say, for what were we but a team of animals pulling in the same direction now that Christ knew G-d's plan for him and I knew G-d's for me?—yoked thus we stumbled blindly forward, goaded by visions of the cross.

The Allele

"I'm out," Jesus said.

"Beg pardon."

"I'm out, I'm done, forget this."

This sudden reversal caught me totally off guard. My so-called temptation of Christ had turned out to be a spectacular failure and little more than an unintended confession. If anyone queered the deal it was G-d and his messenger, John.

"All crown and no cross, huh?"

Jesus slapped me across the face. "Don't be so fucking profane."

"Hey, what's the big idea?"

"I can't do this, this, this … emotional blackmail … of me, of man."

"What'd you expect?"

"An idea worthy of man's dignity. Of my own dignity."

"An *Oration on the Dignity of Man?* Not from Him."

"*Who loves all things as himself.* You get that part?"

"Well, this was always my point.…"

"To think a few years ago I sat at my father's workbench, happy. A genius with a block of wood. Which is enough. To join two pieces of cedar. Or conjure a line of verse. Mix tinctures. Tend flock and field…. But this! To argue the law before man and thus shape his ends. It's immodest, it's im-proper, a fault to man and thus to God—*Who loves all things as himself.* Why He ever put a notion in my head … drew me out of my own obscurity, I'll never know."

"I thought you were keen on this thing: "Alex-andria. Rome." Remember?

"Not like this."

"There's no other way."

"He's … relentless."

"It's in his nature is all, like a gene or line of code; and so it is with our natures, being his heirs—though here's the funny thing: there's something else in the cards that terrifies him, some other I-don't-know-what...."

"So what's the big deal then if he compels us?

"The terms have changed, merely. Where once He compelled our fear, He now compels our love."

"Man, this whole thing stinks like a corporate sellout in the worst way."

"What, you don't want to be in the club?"

"Like some kind of one-hit-wonder who hasn't done a thing in two thousand years, hanging around the after-parties? No thanks."

"The mother of all after-parties, to be fair."

"Times Square New Year's Eve!"

"The Titanic!"

"Branson!"

"Madame Toussalt's!"

"Ha! Imagine me done up in wax."

The idea, little did Jesus know, was not so far from the truth. This iconic Jesus, memorialized on t-shirts, coffee mugs, living room samplers, dashboard figurines, album covers, pendants nestled

amongst chest hair and décolletage and less iron-
ically upon the altar, would live on to the end of
time.

"Which one do you want? The brawling Jesus,
the pensive?" I said.

"Something tasteful."

"*The Pietà,* then. Certainly not upon the cross."

"You decide, Bub."

Despite the levity, Jesus moved forward, always
forward.— You know how it is with a believer, my
friend. They hear you, but they don't really hear you.
Half a dozen times I'd tried to tell Jesus what I
really thought of this G-d. Each time Jesus fell to
complaining about the sentence passed on him,
obdurate in his objections, yet resigned in some
unacknowledged part of himself to its inevitability.
We were coming down the mountain now.

"What the hell do we do now, Beezy."

"Keep walking, Bro."

Church

Strangely, we came upon a Catholic church some-where out in the desert, not a cathedral or one of those chapels on a far-flung Pacific atoll, but like a parish church from the 1940s. Don't ask.

An usher opened the front door, smiling, and led us to an open pew. The family in front turned and smiled as we knelt and crossed ourselves.

"Some strange shit…."

"Shhh," said Jesus.

We sat and waited as parishioners filed in smelling of damp flowers. Then an organist struck up "A Mighty Fortress," wounding my ears slightly, and everyone stood on cue as a little old priest flanked by two altar boys appeared by a series of hidden doorways and circumambulated the congregation, parading, finally, down the nave and mounting the three steps to the altar, right-left-right.

Jesus stared up at the crucifix. His eyes wandered to the stained glass windows and along the vaulted plaster ceiling, then back down to the little priest.

"See that stain in the wall?" Jesus said. "Up there. That's the devil hiding there."

"Is that so?" I said.

"He's most often where he's least wanted … What's *your* name?" he said.

I stared at Jesus, alarmed.

"I'm a good girl," he said.

"The fuck?"

"That's naughty!"

"What's happening?"

The priest bent forward in the pulpit now, towering over the congregation. *"Vade retro Satana!"* he thundered—a bit severely for the Baltimorean assembled, I thought, who sat in their rows placidly thumbing hymnals like nothing out of the ordinary was up; and a single blue flame twirled around the hem of his cassock.

"Who, me?" I said, confused. "No, I don't think I will," I said, regaining my footing.

"Adjure te, spiritus nequisseme, per Deum omnipotentem," spake the priest, gripping the altar rail.

"Come out behind thy sanctuary if thou darest; what you say is all Greek to me."

"Leave this place."

"Nah."

"The power of Christ command thee."

I laughed. "Who, him?" I said, motioning to Jesus. "Little Mary Anne? Why she ain't even bled yet."

The priest gestured to the crucifix hanging behind him.

"Oh, *him,*" I said, pushing my way past somnolent parishioners. "Putting the cart before the horse, somewhat."

"How's that?" said the priest, rolling up his sleeves and stepping into the transept.

"A dead symbol, not yet dead."

"How dare you!" said the priest, turning red in the face.

"Easy." I said. "How dare *you* speak of things you don't properly understand yourself? Soldier of G-d: presume ye to do His bidding who fills thy purse with nine lead farthings and one of gold; step off, a real nigger's in the house."

"How dare you," he sputtered again.

"Anything else?"

"I shall know thee Satan by thy lies."

"Name one."

"You tempted Eve!"

"She was asking for it."

"And the Lord."

"Ditto."

"And man."

"Now man's a funny case … no less in need of temptation than of guidance along the straight-and-narrow. I should think you'd thank me for the gainful employment."

"Don't flatter yourself, bub."

"Funny you should say that, too."

"Hmm?"

"Isn't there something you covet?"

"Don't make me laugh. My life has been one long episode of *Father Ted*. Look about you at these, my flock, arrayed in their Sunday best."

A real southern belle in the third row discretely circled her mouth in cardamine.

"Not even that! No, not that, for am armed with fortitude enough to resist mere pleasures of the flesh, which disgust me, in fact. But look you at those parents worrying over sons and daughters and striving within the bounds of family. How their lives are fraught with purpose; mine a poor imitation of theirs. Avuncular at best…."

"Perhaps best not to romanticize."

" … beset by questions on all sides, yet fortified, as you say, by a single part of knowledge."

"How'd you like a part or two *más?*"

"That is a conundrum."

"It always is."

"I ought to say No."

"Yet have not."

"Stuff my ears with wax."

"Yet have not."

"Renounce thee."

"Yet have not. Say, was that a cock crew?"

"Say, what … have ye got there, anyway? Who…?"

"Why Jesus, naturally. Anything less would be an insult."

"Him?" said the priest, craning his neck to look at Jesus asleep against a column.

"None other."

"Get the fuck out!"

"Now you talk like a regular fellow; see how immediate the change?"

"Nothing's changed, I've agreed to nothing."

"You needn't. Go see for yourself. We've just come from John. I'm afraid he's a bit out of sorts."

"No!" said the priest, astonished.

"In the very flesh and blood. No need to conjure with lots of mumbo-jumbo."

"Say, what's with you, anyway? No sooner do you flatter than you start with the insults."

"Sorry, occupational hazard, I guess."

"No. I'll not examine this Jesus, and be twice tormented. Get the hell out. Please."

"As it pleases your grace," I said, bowing to this most excellent human specimen.— For it so happens that there are such people who are impervious to mischief and other satanic inducements— so much the harder for he, possessed of an historical imagination. The ordinary prole lacks only for curiosity of things beyond his immediate ken; not this man who had painstakingly weened himself from the world on Thomas Aquinas and St. Teresa of Avila, and who slumped now in a chair in the sacristy with a half bottle in his lap and his surplice around his neck like a bib…. (Indeed there is a sweet spot in the human temperament where temptation is concerned.)

"Nice service," Jesus said afterwards, rubbing his eyes.

"Yes."

"Makes one envision the long view."

"Uh-huh."

Outside church the noonday sun emblazoned streets of row houses and corner stores. The green countryside stretched out above a bay.

"What shall we today?" Jesus said, dragging a stick along a white picket fence.

"I've no objection to boiled crab and a bottle of Montrachet."

"That's not kosher."

"We're in the new world, bro."

"Maybe we'd better get back."

A threesome of catholic schoolgirls followed at a distance, giggling.

"You're killing me."

"Look who's talking."

After eluding these pubescents we accosted a cabbie asleep under an old elm tree, drove to the train station and took an Amtrack to DC. Then we caught El Al out of Dulles and in the morning were back in the promised land.

Ministry

We spent a night with Mary, then headed back into the country. Jesus looked about himself, depressed to be home again with nothing more to show for his efforts than a stamp in his passport and a bad case of jet lag. The same groves of date palms, mule tracks and windswept townships seemed to have shrunk beneath the weight of frustrated expectations. And Jesus' imagination lay fallow for a season.

"I think I'd like to go to the shore. I need a break," Jesus said. And so we went down to the sea for a time.

Now there were those who spent their days about these shores. Simon-Peter … John … Bartholomew. I couldn't keep the bastards straight. Dirty fishermen all, they'd tell their wives they were heading out and then go on a bender for the next three days, drinking and dicing and sleeping under overturned boats. For some reason Jesus gravitated to these types, perhaps construing in their rustic simplicity a virtuousness of some sort; or else wanting to abase himself and so make an unworthy vessel of G-d. Whatever reason, Jesus hung around, trying with increasing recklessness to ingratiate himself with these fools. It started with harmless dares: "Dive off that rock, swim out to that break."

Jesus obliged, swimming out as far as he could, then fighting exhaustion the whole way back. Once, twice he went under, the fisherman stirring uneasily on the beach, but each time Jesus resurfaced, swimming hard until exhaustion overtook him again and his arms made sluggish movements in the waves. Then he went under a third time and did not reappear. The fisherman waited for what seemed a reasonable time, then looking each to the other, simultaneously went scrambling into the water, thrashing about and calling and finding him finally, hauled him out and pumped his lungs until Jesus came around again.

"Jesus returns from the dead," he sputtered, giving me a wink. And the fisherman—The Apostles he'd grown fond of calling them—hoisted Jesus onto their shoulders and carried him about the beach, making up snatches of song as they went: "Jesus of the deep, return to us on the tide…."

He became quite the favorite, actually, in the way that an outsider may become a favorite by flattering the insider's sense of himself; though in the bitter end, when push comes to shove, a stranger.

Many days wore on in this way, and Jesus grew strong in mind and body. He was happy, I think, and without realizing it, as so often happens, had begun to lay a groundwork on which he might build his case—for it had not occurred to him that he might gather those about him who shared his concerns.

Here was John, poet manque, ready to summarize with a phrase; and Philip, full of a passionate intensity that faltered whenever someone contradicted him; Thomas was an exceedingly careful fellow whose family made small loans to tradesmen; and Bartholomew, possessed of an exceptional mind, much to his own chagrin amongst these country fellows who valued readiness over reflection and who indeed regarded anything other than reckless abandon as cowardice; and lastly Simon-Peter, whose own uxoriousness was really a key to the rest, playing the outlaw and kicking the sand with big black boots, while in private returning each night to his wife, whom he cherished beyond all else.

In sum, each of these personalities was shaped by frustration with the forces that conspired to make their lives hard. These were good men, who if they spoke harshly, did so regretting that they did not know how to speak nicely; who if they cut up rough at the pub, hectoring a tourist or jostling the jukebox, were certain to show up the next morning to make amends; and who if they were treated unjustly by their overlords bowed their heads obsequiously and only grumbled in private.

On days they went out, Jesus would stand at the bow of the boat and stare across the water.

"Down in front," one of the men quipped.

"Quiet!" Jesus reprimanded. "Look to that shore. What place is that?"

"Capernaum? I know a girl there," Simon said.

"Her misfortune I suppose, eh, Petros?" Jesus said.

"Hardly.— Call me Simon."

"If you say so, Peter."

Simon-Peter gripped a gunnel and rocked the boat.

"Darest me to walk upon the waves, Simon? I'll do it," Jesus said.

"Somehow I doubt thee not … Call me Peter, though. Strangely, the way you say it suits."

At Capernaum they landed the boat and climbed a hill to a little black basalt synagogue. Inside was damp and cool. A dim light filtered through an opening in the roof illuminating unplastered walls and hidden niches. It was a modest room built to human scale, a place amidst this world of gods and devils where a man might abide according to his own needs and passions, and perhaps at length prosper.

Jesus turned in a circle, looking up at the ceiling. A delighted grin broke out on his face, and he sat on a stone bench against a wall and let out a long sigh. "And so it begins," he said.

Roadhouse

For the next weeks we stayed at this place, the fishermen coming and going, drawn again and again to this Jesus, who seemed to find his direction amidst the aimlessness all around him.

"See how Peter slips out each night and rows home before his wife's awake?" Jesus said. "How long can a man go on like that before he gets burnt?"

"That one's pussywhipped for sure," said Philip, and the apostles laughed aloud, each one the louder for the guiltiness in his own heart.

"Is it any different for the man who goes to God on the Sabbath, then runs off with the Devil on Wednesday?"

"What would you have us do, Jesus? We have business."

"What business is that, John, sleeping under an overturned boat? … *I* propose a bit of business."

"What business is that?"

"Why, God's business ye wretched, whose business is the world."

"This world that trods us underfoot?"

"Aye. This world, which we shall turn upside down and inside out like a purse until the last farthing's been shaken out."

"Mean we should go a-robbing?"

"No, for a thief takes what is not theirs. The thing that we shall go a-robbing belongs to all men. 'Twas taken from thee at birth without thy knowing."

"Yes, yes!" said these world-weary apostles, no strangers to injustice, who daily suffered the indignities of harbor master, game warden, fish merchant and tax collector, and going home each evening, ashamed, imagined indignities anew.

"For I tell you, Ye shall be a light unto the world."

Yet Peter was still with doubt. "I have a family, a life."

"Whoever loves his life shall lose it, and whoever loses his life shall save it."

"Yeah, I never understood that."

"What do you figure your life is worth, Peter?"

"Cannot quantify it."

"So not figured in shekels?"

"No."

"That's good. For there is another currency by which a man may value his life. I speak of cause and of righteous action."

"What cause?"

"Why, that is for each man to decide for himself. Our cause concerns justice. And if a man, throwing his coin onto the scale, reckons he may tip the balance, why then 'tis character that compels him to throw in."

"Let me ask you this," John cut in. "How do we know that we're not just throwing after another *lost* cause?"

"Better you ask yourself, John."

"But how can we be guaranteed of success?" asked Thomas.

"What success do you seek, Thomas?"

"Why, victory; destruction of mine enemy."

"Such victories are fleeting, Thomas. Did not the House of David fall to the Pharaohs? Egypt to the Assyrians? The Assyrians to Babylon? Come Nebuchadnezzar, Darius, Alexander, Herod. Indeed, we have no such army as those, nor strive for a plot of earth merely, but for the everlasting truth that shines within man's soul."

"Have we that truth?"

"Have we not, Peter? Look within you."

"But a sign…." said Mathew.

"A sign?" said Jesus. "That's the stuff of fairy tales."

"No, a sign would be good," said Peter.

"Yes, traditionally, one wants some sort of sign," said John.

"Want you a sign? Why look here," Jesus said, unbuttoning his shirt, wearied of the skepticism, the hedging, the pragmatism and the superstition of these men: "Look you at this little iron cross. 'Twas given by the Devil, who rules *his* kingdom— and that lost portion of men's souls—for all time."

A Sign

I'd gone to Bethsaida on a bit of business—one can tolerate so much fraternity—and coming back across the water spied a crowd gathered in the town square above the bay. Capernaum lay along a Roman supply route. A military train had stopped over in the noon heat. Among the scarlet tunics many white garments were crowded, and I urged the boatman on, anxious to see what could be the matter.

A Sign

As I climbed the hill to the town I heard muffled shouts, and cresting the top saw through the legs of the many gathered an animal leaping about. A full grown lioness, grown increasingly agitated, nipped and curvetted at a man. The man, his arm wrapped in a bloody garment, feinted toward the beast, then leaped back, feinted and leaped back again. Then he dropped his arms at his side and looked skyward. (Oh, Jesus.)

"Behold, *Agnus Dei,*" Jesus shouted above the din. "The lamb of God, like a lamb led to slaughter … Well," he said a level lower, swaggering about the circle, "not today." And he leaped at the beast, baring his teeth. And the lioness leaped back at him. And the two embraced and rolled in the dust.

The lioness came out on top, but Jesus kicked it off, and the lion backed away. Then Jesus got to his feet to a great roaring from the crowd. "I tell you, he who follows me shall not die…."

I watched, rivetted, wondering not how Jesus would manage the beast, which was wandering in confused circles lashing its tail, but how he would manage the rhetorical figure of his relation to G-d. His theology whipsawed back and forth so this last year.

"He who follows me shall taste everlasting life, for I herald one greater—*who loves all things as himself,*" and so saying Jesus turned and smirked at me.

Could it be, I wondered with amazement, that he'd worked out the problem of G-d with that simple smirk? Had swept aside the entire question of free-will with a single, ironic gesture? Had placed himself outside the very limits of scripture and Talmud and so set himself an authority? Had, as he'd so presciently guessed, constructed his own web?

Jesus advanced toward the lion, which seemed to have lost interest in the proceeding. He advanced again, and the lion moved away at an angle.

A centurion stepped forward and prodded the animal with his spear. The lioness took one savage swipe at the weapon and trotted back into its cage, turned twice and settled down to licking its paws like a great house cat.

In the center of the ring Jesus addressed the assembled: "You have seen for yourselves. Great are the ways of God. Great is his instrument."

A brazier heaped with smoking coals was dragged into the square and the disciples hauled a net full of fish from a cart. Local merchants brought loaves of bread, olives, figs and goat cheese. And Simon-Peter hung a great goatskin filled with wine from his family vineyard on an iron hook.

During the feasting Jesus moved off by himself, and I joined him on a precipice overlooking the lake. The water shimmered with the last light of day. Then a breeze rippled the water, making purple shadows.

"That was satisfactory," I said.

"They wanted a sign," he said.

"Gave you?"

"I guess," he said.

I had a whiff of vinegar. "You piss yourself?"

"Yeah," Jesus said.

Sermon on the Mount

Now the disciples were much impressed with what they had seen, and Jesus sought to disabuse them of their appetite for cheap thrills alone. The next morning Jesus rose early and roused those gathered: Simon-Peter, Phillip, Bartholomew, John, et. al., and led them on a walkabout.

"Arise, ye idlers. Daylight upon the plain!" Jesus shouted.

And they followed Jesus across a vast outback, rubbing their eyes and dragging their bedding behind them in wet grass.

"Where are you taking us?" asked Bartholomew, shyly.

"Those hills, better before the sun's overhead," said Jesus, and feeling he might strike a more vatic note, added, "… lest we become the Sunday roast."

Our little crowd straggled along, followed by a little donkey cart. Soon we struck up a brisk tempo, around mid-morning fell into a jog and as the noon sun rose its hammer sprinted the last mile to the shade of some acacia trees at the foot of a mount.

"Let's rest here a minute," Jesus said, and we sprawled out in a sweaty heap, arms and legs akimbo, as the day's last heat boiled off the plain.

A cock crew in the upper branches of a tree and we started awake.

"Alive?" said Jesus.

"Unfortunately," said John.

"Then let us seek our fortunes somewhere else," Jesus said. "Follow me to the top of this little hill." And Jesus began a swift ascent of the mountain.

The sun set as we reached the summit, and the western hills glowed like embers of a dying fire. A breeze stirred and the first stars appeared in the sky. Then a damp mist blew over the hill, causing us to shiver as Jesus began to speak.

"Listen," he said, as the disciples drew near, "so that you might remember what I have to say."

"Think not too much of yourselves, for you are but atoms in infinity. Nor think too little, for all infinity is contained within thee, you dig?"

Jesus started strong, if not in a slightly mystical vein.

"Think not of thy comfort nor thy reputations, which are a poor cushion, indeed. Nor think of what has passed, nor to come, for all things pass back and forth, through thee.

"But make a channel of yourselves, so that the tides may enter thee and flow back out, dredging thee and arranging thee according to their whim; yet mindful, ye fishermen, of thine own purpose.

"Fear not that thou shall be unequal to thy task, for the Lord shall not place so much in your net, nor so little that ye shall find yourselves without; yet finding yourselves surfeited, throw a portion back; and lacking, set something aside.

"Keep custom, for you may find in the simplicity of home a bulwark against a howling at thy doorstep. And in thy homes, honor each simple thing: cradle, fork, footstool, for all things are holy. Use them thus.

Jesus paused and considered these words, understanding that his homely phrases were perhaps overfamiliar with his audience, who needed no such exhortations to modesty. And he swerved:

"Nor waste a moment contemplating any of these, for they are but shadows of the true self, which runs naked before thee …"

This struck a chord.

" … Rather, keep apace of thy lives afore they outrun thee; and accosting thyself, demand to know not what thou *mayest,* but what thou *wilt.*"

The apostles stirred now.

"Discover what greatness is in thee."

"Hear, hear," they said.

"Take that greatness and bend it to thy purpose."

"Yes!"

"Purpose thyselves, then, yea task thyselves, to do something extraordinary … remembering that each life is extraordinary, each step, each breath extraordinary, and what may be accomplished within its compass extraordinary."

"Nice save," I said afterwards.

"I thought so," said Jesus.

Indeed, this "sermon" became a favorite among the disciples, who were oft heard exhorting one another afterwards: "What wilt thou, Phillip?" "What wilt *thou,* John?" … *"Wilt* thou, Peter?" "Aye, *wilt!"* and so on.

(Of course Jesus said a good many other things about lilies of the fields and closets and so forth, and I leave it to those gospels that tell of such things to enumerate them. In them one finds testimony of Jesus' devotion to G-d, [if not the author's own devotion]. What they omit is Jesus' devotion to *life* and his thorough involvement in the day-to-day of Judea. Such banalities are a mere foreground to greater doings in the gospels of Mathew and John et. al. Unnamed beggars and cripples are mere stepping stones to Jesus' apotheosis. This is not what Jesus taught. Therefore, let this humble gospel lend some color to those scenes whose omission is a *biographical* sin at least.

Barn Raising

We camped upon the mountain and in the morn stopped in a grove of cedars. Jesus produced an axe from the donkey cart that we'd left along the trail.

"Easy to tear down, but to build is the work of man. Let us take a dozen of these into town," Jesus said, and the disciples took up the axe and felled and dressed a dozen of the tallest cedars and loaded them onto the cart.

A full day we hauled and shoved the little cart across the plain and into Capernaum. The next day we arrived at the property of Josephus, whose house had burnt down. When we arrived, Josephus was sifting through the ashes while his wife and daughters sat in the shade of a single sheet strung between two bushes mending what might.

"Yea, Josephus," Jesus called.

"Know me, sir?" Josephus replied.

"Aye, Josephus," said Jesus.

"I don't think I know thee," said Josephus.

"Knowest thou the Lord God?" Jesus said.

"Aye, in my heart," said Josephus.

"Then I know thee," Jesus said, approaching. And he grasped Josephus' hand firmly in his own. "Let us rake these ashes aside, for they are of no worth; yet there is a foundation beneath that we shall build upon." And the disciples fell to raking and sweeping. Then timbers were laid out and a frame set up and by dusk a roofbeam hauled into place.

In the waning daylight Jesus sat astride the beam singing and hammering, and the sound of his joy echoed through the valley.

Barn Raising

The next morn a crowd appeared, for word had spread of this barn raising. One by one they brought what they could spare: wood scraps, thatch, pots and pans, a mattress and much-mended garments, and by nightfall Josephus and his family took shelter in their new abode.

In the yard, Jesus spoke: "Let us leave Josephus and his family on this happy reestablishment of their house—yea, their *home,* for though we have resurrected wood and thatch, I tell you that the spirit, too, may be raised from ashes."

And the apostles, greatly weary of limb, hauled the little donkey cart back to the synagogue.

"A lot of work just to make a point," I said afterwards.

"A point is easily made," Jesus said. "The work's the point."

"Sure."

"Just thought I should say something afterwards … while I have breath."

The apostles continued in this way about Judea, building and husbanding, gathering and mending with nary a thought for themselves, for a fisherman of all men is a factotum: a carpenter, a navigator, a weatherman, a seamstress, a nurse, a preacher.

And it came to pass that the little church at Capernaum became a hub of activity, and with that activity attached a certain moral authority so that sometimes people came to Jesus with their disputes. These Jesus heard reluctantly, though adjudicated decisively.

Most were civil in nature, involving a boundary or a beast. Jesus was careful to usurp Roman authority. Yet there was a case involving a woman who'd been mistreated by her husband. The families arrived at the synagogue in a state of great agitation.

"My son-in-law has much abused my Barbara," the father began, gesturing to a young man with a bouffant.

The wife, a small athletic girl with green eyes, stood behind her father.

"Has beat her for no reason."

Jesus came out from behind his little table.

"Why, kept her out of doors last night," the father said.

The boy's father stepped forward. "'Tis my son's wife, lawfully, to do with as he pleases. Why her old man beat her the same."

"A lie!"

"Why no lie, I bought her for six bushels and an ox."

"A bull!" cried the girl's father.

Jesus looked to the young couple, one to the other. "What say ye?"

"That bitch!" cried the boy.

The girl smirked to herself.

"Will have her obey me. She's mine!"

"'Tis mine!" yelled the father. "I raised her."

And Jesus spoke. "What do you have to say, girl? Barbara, is it? Come girl, step forward."

The girl stepped forward and spoke thus. "Why, I belong to no one; I belong to myself."

"And so say?"

"Shall stay with thee," said the girl, to a great consternation in the crowd.

"So be it," said Jesus.

"No!" the husband's family cried.

"No!" cried her father.

"Thus!" cried Jesus.

The litigants rushed forward, but the disciples closed ranks, blocking the way, and the crowd surged from the galley and routed those families from the yard and down the street and out of town.

This Barbara, then, became the thirteenth. And she cut her hair and bound her breasts, and wearing fisherman's jeans joined the rough life of the Synagogue.

Court

As a result of aforementioned judgement, a steady stream of plaintiffs paraded their grievances before us. It seemed that this semblance of a court had loosed some long unrequited thirst for justice in the township, and pretty soon all our time was spent hearing slip-and-falls and foreclosures; and Jesus shortly lost his temper with these litigious Judeans. In the end I think he was on the verge of a nervous breakdown before we hauled him away. Some of his decisions were pretty hilarious, though.

"What we have here," Jesus spoke with mock gravity, "is a case that concerns us all. Why, if a man should slip on a banana peel in the grocery aisle, what might the state? By what negligence might the whole system be laid low? And what scale measure such great loss of consortium? Why, today a banana, tomorrow Judea! I find for the plaintiff. A banana. Next!"

As the crowd was dispersing, I found Jesus slumped in his chambers.

"Have neither the wisdom of Solomon nor the patience of Job," he said, passing a hand over his brow. "Indeed, one almost pities these magistrates who spend their lives divining a droplet of truth in a drought of lies … and find I care not. Care not! No, not for these petty squabbles. Why woulds't throw sand in the very gears of justice!"

It grieved me so to find Jesus in this state. "Let go, Jesus," I said. "Let be what must. 'Tis this very tension that holds the world in place: the warden's job to incarcerate, the convict's to escape. This I know quite well. Why, I thought thee did, too."

"I forget what I'm doing, Beezy."

"Keep to thy business, bro."

"What business is that?"

"Why, man's soul, remember?"

"Man's sole?" said Jesus, "which trods upon the dirt and must soon be replaced?"

"Now that's a very witty fellow," I said and slapped him twice across the face. "Been waiting for the chance to even the score, by the way."

Jesus laughed and then snivelled a little. "What's the point of all this Beezy?"

"Not to belabor the point: man's soul."

"And yet find I come to wonder at its worth. What's it worth?"

"Man's soul? To me, a lark as individuals go. In sum … something more."

"See, I'd say the opposite were true. *En masse* the object is fairly indistinct. Individually, 'tis man's dearest possession."

"Will certainly pay dearly in its exchange, I've found; and yet I confess, I don't believe man has a soul, or whatever you call it.… "

"Why 'tis nothing more than a man's conception of himself."

"That's fair."

"His inherent sense of dignity."

'Like that man with the banana?"

"Oh, him. Spied a-swinging his cane in the hall and dancing on all the black tiles. The devil take him!"

"Not so fast! Hell's full of song-and-dance men. You have to have real talent—*soul*, you might say—which comes at a price."

"What price?"

"Why pain of death. *Duende,* I've heard it called."

"Now this is somewhat out of my area."

"*Au contraire!* Who ever waltzed into heaven without a care in the world? Don't think the down escalator is any different than the up!"

"You exasperate me, Beelzebub."

"Good, that's what I'm here for."

A Diablolical Piece
of Reasoning

In the end, there came before the court a herdsman who had sold a ram for ten bushels. The receiver gladly took the beast and sent it out to pasture to mate with his ewes, but when none got with kid, it became clear that the animal was impotent; so the receiver demanded to be recompensed. The herdsman refused, saying that such things are not foreseeable, and the receiver began to slander him throughout the town. "This man is a common thief, a *gonef!*" complained the man to whomever would listen. "Why sold me a dam with horns, damn him." The scandalmongering reached comic proportions when he drove the beast through town in a dress.

At some point the herdsman relented and offered pennies on the dollar, but the receiver, carried away by his sense of injustice, only increased his campaign of abuse. When at last the receiver began to malign the herdsman in the local press, the herdsman sued for libel.

Came these before Jesus.

"This man has spoken falsely against me," began the herdsman.

"Sold me a worthless ram," interrupted the receiver.

"Why, you looked him in the mouth yourself."

"'Tis not the mouth that's the trouble."

"Not my fault you don't know one end from the other."

"Not my fault you don't know your own trade."

"A-know my trade."

"A-know you're a knave!"

"Here, here, why he defames me right here in court."

"No lie, your honor, the man's a knave!"

"Should thrash you...."

"Try it."

"Bailiff!" called Jesus. "Remove these men."

And a couple of local toughs whom we'd deputized to keep the peace led the men outside.

Jesus sat back in his chair and looked up at the ceiling, and the disciples murmured amongst themselves in the gallery.

"Shall rule for the herdsman," said Phillip.

"How so?" said Bartholomew. "Sold him defective goods."

"But the charge is libel," said John.

"'Tis no libel to demand repayment," said Bartholomew.

"But to sully a man's good name," said Phillip.

"Ach, what name? Who's he?" said John.

"To him is everything," said Phillip.

Jesus called the bailiffs to return the men to court. "What else?" Jesus said.

"What else?" said the men. "Why nothing else. 'Tis all."

"You're satisfied, then, having presented your case in the eyes of God and man? A bum steer from you, and a lot of nonsense from you?"

"Your honor?"

"Nay, there's no honor in it. Bailiffs, take these men out back and give them some lashes, damnit. Dismissed."

A minor cry went up in the court as the men were led outside, and the disciples accosted Jesus in his chambers.

"Well, this doesn't seem right at all—to punish both?" "A-came here seeking justice!"

The crack of a whip was heard outside and a low moan.

"Justice?" said Jesus. "These men love not justice, but love only themselves."

Another crack of the whip, followed by a yelp.

"Fear they not the law, but only ill-repute."

Later, I caught Jesus alone at the synagogue. "A diabolical piece of reasoning," I said, "Congratulations."

"The Devil's not so black," said Jesus, "or Jesus so white. Cans't not paint a canvas all one color. That's a wall."

A Whale

Now the next morning we waited at the court, but no one showed. Nor the next morning, nor the next after that. In fact, no one ever showed again. Though people in secret applauded Jesus decision to have both men flogged—as they were both generally disliked in town, no less so for their interminable feuding—everyone thought twice now before trotting spurious claims before Jesus … which was just fine with us, no more rationalizations, no more lies, no more lawyering….

It being fine weather, we quit the court and went a-sailing it so happened.

A fair breeze blew down from the hills and the fishermen's lateen sails flitted like butterflies above the green waves. Jesus, Peter and Barbara sailed upon Peter's bark; Mathew and John in another; Thomas and James upon Thomas' boat; and Philip and Bartholomew upon another, curving into one another's paths.

"Starboard tack!" hollered John, racing before Thomas.

"Let out the sheet," cried James.

The jockeying done, we fell into place and headed on a beam reach out to sea. Here, beyond the breakwater, the sea grew dark and raised the little boats up and dropped them down in stately swells.

Barbara held Jesus' hand. "Have you someone, Jesus?" she asked.

"There was one."

"Where is she now?"

"Back in Jerusalem."

"What happened?"

"I left."

"That's sad."

"Is it?" said Jesus, staring toward the horizon.

"Well, no. I think much is made of these things."

"I might have stayed, you know, but I think she preferred it this way."

"I see."

"What about you?"

"Oh, there was a moment, when he was captain of the soccer team and I was just a sophomore, and I just *had* to have him. Afterwards — it's funny, you know that poem about the swan? 'Did she put on his knowledge with his power before the indifferent beak could let her drop?' — Afterwards I realized I wanted no part of that; I knew myself already. What more's to know?— But, you know, in the country things take their course."

"I'm glad you're here with us, Barbara."

"I'm glad, too, Jesus, because honestly you all could stand a little feminine perspective."

Jesus laughed. And then he stood in the boat and sang out, "A whale! Methinks I see a whale!"

Indeed, the great, barnacled flank of a humpback rose out of the water and then slid beneath the surface like some great sea slug, then a hundred yards distant spouted a jet of mist.

Thomas and James trimmed their sail in pursuit.

As if in a game of hide-and-seek the whale dove and then surfaced at random intervals, here between the boats, there many yards distant.

Now, it is a strange undertaking to spend time with a beast. Only after many years with an animal may one come to truly know its moods and its habits, its desire for companionship and its desire for solitude. It's sorrows and joys….

The whale surfaced off the bow of Jesus' boat and rolled over so that its great eye, as big as a dinner plate, stared unblinking up at Jesus.

Jesus, grasping the spar, leaned far over the waves and gazed back at the whale, which dove and resurfaced at the stern. The whale played at this game, diving back and forth under the boat, whilst Jesus scrambled from side to side; then it breached full out of the water and sent a great wave over the gunnels, nearly swamping us. And then it dove deep and returned no more.

Jesus grinned the way back—that same grin the first day I'd seen him. And Barbara stripped off her shirt and unwound the tight bandage that rightly pained her breasts and lay fully nude upon the deck in the sun's warmth.

A Whale

When they landed on the beach Jesus talked excitedly, and the fishermen indulged him, having themselves seen every manner of thing upon the sea; and Jesus obliged *them,* whom he felt, suddenly, he'd spent too much time haranguing.

"'Tis a good omen it didn't thrash thee with its flukes," said Thomas, laughing.

"Aye?"

"Have seen!"

"Yea, and some are mean and full of guile as any human," said John.

"'Tis true?" said Jesus.

" … Only there's a kind of honesty they require, being what they are," spoke Bartholomew, shyly, from his habitual place outside the circle.

"That's interesting, Bartholomew."

"Well, yes."

"Like the innocents."

"To be with them is to trust oneself," Bartholomew said with a finality, turning away from the others.

Jesus meditated on these words as they marched home and decamped at the little synagogue, amazed at the profound insights in the mouths of these ordinary fishermen, who if they little understood

the deeper meaning of their words, were yet possessed of a native intelligence just the same. And
like a child nestled between his parents, Jesus fell
into a dreamless sleep.

Winter

When the rainy season came we hauled the fishing boats above the wrack and bolted the front door of the synagogue. A low fire smoldered in the corner of the room, and the disciples huddled together, speaking in low voices.

Jesus took the Torah from its little cupboard and began to read the verses aloud, stopping here and there to question the disciples.

"What meanest here when says, *Let there be light*"? Jesus said.

"Why, 'twas God lighting the heavens," said Paul.

"Ostensibly, yes," said Jesus, letting the matter lie, for wondered how he might reveal unto these earnest disciples a deeper subject; and grasping the page between thumb and forefinger tore it from the book and fed it into the fire—and thus continued over many days and weeks, reading the pages and tearing them out and dropping them into the fire.

In the halo of light one spied the various countenances of the disciples: John, in a distracted way, arranging his own words; Bartholomew deep in thought; Peter captivated by some fleeting heroic ideal; Thomas shocked and affrighted.

A deep contentment shone in Jesus' aspect. This domestic life at the synagogue brought out some profound part of his nature. Each evening as he prepared the daily meal, baking bread and portioning out salted fish and olives, he joked with those disciples over inane matters.— Was in fact a gifted impressionist and would single out one disciple or another to mimic:

"Jesus lifted up the world upon his back," said Jesus, feverishly writing in a book. "Why healed the lepers and wrote Stairway to Heaven," he said, lumbering about and hectoring the others like John....

"My wife!" he cried, running about in a feverish circle. And the disciples broke into uproarious laughter, pounding Peter upon the chest.

And lastly, strutting imperiously about the stage: "May I offer you a cigarette? There is much I have yet to tell, but, oh, how weary ... My shirt? Why found it at Barneys upon the sale-rack!"

"Oh, funny man!" I yelled above the din. Let me give you this, I said, taking the stage, and raising forefinger to temple: "Let us not into temptation," I said in a whisper. "Oh G-d no, not that! ... But being more or less constantly tempted—nudge-nudge, wink-wink—let us go about that business—indeed, such business as shallt have ... yea, as *have*, and as *have had* ... and thus having—business, I mean, shall do that bidding, having thus, wait, what?"

The apostles laughed with all the delight of hearing a forbidden joke. I went on a little recklessly, to great applause, "And thus having!...."

"Jesus, do I sound like that?" Jesus said afterwards.

"Just a little."

*

Now if the disciples slumbered through many rainy days, chewing their food and nodding their heads, so too did that part of their imaginations that reckons with time slumber, for they went about without a care for the next hour or minute, even as time sped toward them with all its pre-arranged events....

When they finally reached the end of the book, Jesus fed the last folio into the fire and the boards, too, so that there was nothing left, save an acrid, antique smell.

"And so we arrive at the end of history," Jesus said, "free to write the next chapter ourselves."

John perked up.

"The law of Moses was meant to guide Moses' generation," Jesus said, pausing for effect. "The word of Jesus shall guide his. Therefore, let us strike a new covenant with God. Though nothing that Jesus says lies outside the teaching of the fathers, yet shall it deepen their relationship with God as in a marriage in which mutual love shall supersede any thought of duty." Here Jesus glanced toward Barbara in acknowledgment of all the things she had to say about marriage and about love.

"Yea, let us divine God's intentions: If God loves man, then so shall I love man. But if I hate man, then so shall I hate God. Yea, if I speak against a man, then I speak against God. And if I strike a man, I strike God."

Now the disciples were much astonished, who knowing Jesus all along were certainly aware of his insight, yet had no conception to date of the breadth of his philosophy, nor what it demanded of them.

And here Bartholomew spoke up: "Yes, if I do injury to another man, I do injury to God … and injuring God, do injure myself."

And Jesus knelt before Bartholomew, saying, "Peace be with you Bartholomew. Of all, you have understood."

The Lepers' Colony

In spring, when clement weather returned, Judea dragged its collective household out-of-doors to drive the dampness from moldy pillows and mattresses. And above the town in caves carved into the rock, those poor Lepers brought out their own rags.

"Let us climb up to those caves," Jesus said to the disciples, "where those pariahs hide themselves away, and let us see if we may ease their suffering in some way, for I tell you: No thing in God's creation shall remain hidden from the sight of the Lord." And gathering clean linens and herbs we made the long trek uphill.

At the entrance to one of these caves we were met by a man whose nose seemed crushed into his face.

"What business do you men have here?" The man spoke with difficulty, dabbing with a horrid little rag at the mucous that constantly ran into his mouth. "We are under quarantine."

"No business," spoke Jesus, "for seek nothing in return."

"'Tis no place, here," said the man.

"Are nothing ourselves," said Jesus.

"Well, then, come and sit and we shall speak of nothing."

And the disciples sat in the sunlight outside the entrance of a cave. At length several men came shuffling out of the darkness, shielding their eyes from the light.

"This here is Saul and this Solomon. Am called Syrus."

"I am Jesus. Here's John and Bartholomew. This one's Beelzebub."

"Enchante," I said, touching match to cigarette to keep the effluvium from my nose.

"Oh, have not had one of those in such a long time," said Syrus.

"Smoke?"

"Aye."

"Well here, have this one," I said, handing over the cigarette, which he grasped with difficulty between the stubs of his fingers.

"Nor I," said Solomon.

"Or I," said Saul.

So we reclined in the cave's mouth on a broken bed of shale as if on the most sumptuous couch, blowing smoke rings at the ceiling.

"How many are you?" asked Jesus.

"A few dozen," said Syrus. "But they are mostly bedridden, or so disfigured they would not fain show themselves."

"With your permission—and theirs—we desire to wash and to dress your wounds."

Syrus laughed and was seized by a fit of coughing which rattled the contagion in his lungs. "You've strange desires."

"Aye. Am driven by strange desires."

"As you wish, but be warned, you'll not like what you see."

Now the disciples set up a hospital. Thomas and Phillip boiled water whilst Barbara tore the linen into bandages, and John, Bartholomew and Peter went with Jesus into the cave, carrying a single torch whose flame stood straight up in the motionless air.

As they made their way into the recesses, the air thickened with damp mineral smells, human odors and the reek of putrefaction, and the disciples wound bandages around their faces, struck to a man by the irony that they should veil themselves before these disfigured.

In those days one knew about leprosy—had perhaps glimpsed some poor soul in an alley or hospital ward, turning quickly away to blot out the indelible image—yet were no less frightened by the disease for its familiarity. Of all the human maladies it cruelly marks the sufferer. For all those inner torments that blights man's soul, the leper wears his affliction on his sleeve, a constant reminder for all to see.

Now all at once many human faces appeared from the darkness, huddled in corners and half standing.

"Peace be with you," said Jesus.

"And with you," came a voice from the darkness.

"Pray, we bring medicines and bandages. Whoever wishes our assistance, please call out."

There was a long silence.

"Aye," came a voice finally. And a man swung himself forward on his hands and arse, his legs eaten away to the knee, the stumps wrapped in old rags that themselves had become enmeshed with the rotting flesh.

"What is thy name?"

"Jedidah."

"Come Jedidah, and make thyself comfortable." And Jesus bid the disciples bring a bowl of water. Then John rushed out of the cave, overcome.

"Cans't not! Oh God!" he cried aloud outside the cave, "Cans't not!" so that Barbara fetched a bowl of the boiling water and joined the others in his place.

The man, Jedidah, reclined on a mound of dirt as they mixed neem and other oils into the steaming water and slowly submerged his stumps. And at length they disentangled the old rags from the flesh. Then they dabbed at the wounds, pulling away bits of dead flesh.

"Hold still," Jesus said.

"No problem. The feeling's gone. Though cannot say one ever gets used to the idea of losing another piece...."

Jesus applied a poultice and began bandaging the wound. "What were you in life, Jedidah?"

"A carpenter."

"Me, too!"

"Oh, it's good work. I miss that as much as anything, feeling as if one has something useful to do."

"What do you do here?"

"Bury the dead mostly."

"'Tis useful."

"Will do."

"Myself am preparing a grave."

"Whose?"

"Mine own, in fact."

"'Tis strange."

"Yes, and I tell you this only because you shall not see for yourself, though perhaps have news of the world from time to time: They shall persecute me in town. Accuse me of blasphemy. And of healing lepers and other incredible things. Though in truth thou hast healed me ... and so shall be remembered for thy patience with my own vain efforts and thy name written down." And Jesus placed his hand on the Jedidah's neck and lay his forehead against Jedidah's.

Likewise, the disciples ministered to many others with equally ghastly wounds. When the last man had been attended to, the disciples burnt the unclean rags and washed themselves. Then Syrus approached once more.

"There is one more," Syrus said gravely. And Jesus followed him back into the cave, where a shadow swayed in a recess in the rock.

"Come forward, if you please," said Jesus, and a woman stepped into the flickering light carrying a bundle.

"My child is yet unafflicted, methinks," she said.

The woman's face was clear and the skin on her hands unblemished, but she moved with a peculiar twisting motion in her hip; and the woman knelt painfully before Jesus holding out the child and shedding many tears.

Jesus faltered, overcome with emotion. "Oh, woman, thou shallt break my heart!"

"Take him. Please," the woman sobbed. "Take my little Mark." And Barbara rushed forward and knelt before the woman and held out her arms. And she took the child, pulling gently so that the woman finally relinquished her grip and so doing let out a piercing cry that echoed deep into the cave.

Jesus remained standing, stunned, struggling with a desire to smash his fists into the rock. Then Syrus and Solomon gathered the woman to her feet and led her into the darkness.

Outside the cave, they examined the child and washed him and swaddled him in clean linens. And Barbara snatched the child up, and unwrapping the linen around her breasts held him close.

"What do ye intend?" said John, blocking her way.

"Intend to take the child with us," said Barbara.

"Cans't not!" said John. "You heard those men. 'Tis under quarantine."

"Be damned!" A fierce light glimmered in her eye.

"'Tis right," said Peter. "Why, might infect many more."

"Be damned!" said Barbara, looking wildly about her. And John reached out to pry the baby away.

"Let go you coward!" shouted Barbara. And here Bartholomew stepped forward.

"Let go, John. Shall Barbara decide."

"Is that right, Bartholomew?" said John, challenging him. "You stepping up, now?"

"Aye, John," said Bartholomew, shoving John roughly away.

"Alright, now, little bookworm," said John, rolling up a sleeve.

"Peace, you disciples!" spoke Jesus, returning to his senses. "What price a single child? Why, if cannot save a child, cannot save the world." And Barbara stood beside Jesus, fiercely clutching this child whom she would guard the rest of her days and bring up as her very own.

Yet John and Bartholomew scoffed at one another.

"Virgin!" cried John.

"Oaf," said Bartholomew.

And the disciples sorted themselves accordingly on the way back to Capernaum, silently battered by many emotions: indeed right sorrowful for the sufferings of those unfortunates in the caves; doubtful of this child that they had rescued; yet for the most part joyful to escape, themselves, into the light of day.

Paul

This disputation between John and Bartholomew spilled into the open back at Capernaum, threatening our *esprit de corps*. Each minor question put to the group found the two at odds and were oft heard bickering in private.

"Speak you for Jesus?" Bartholomew said to John.

"I know his mind," said John.

"Yet knowest not thine own," said Bartholomew.

"Now what's that supposed to mean?"

"I see how you go running off to your friend."

"What business is that of yours?"

"'Tis all our business, whose thoughts and actions are portrayed in garish fashion by this fool."

"A little artistic license."

"Lies."

"Callest me a liar, Bartholomew?"

"Aye, and a dangerous fool."

Now the two came to blows, and John being the much larger man gave Bartholomew a clout. Loathe to watch this bullying I stepped between.

"Break it up now. There," I said, putting the squeeze on John so that his eyes widened in disbelief and a veil dropped from some part of his imagination, and seeing me for the moment unvarnished, fled....

"What's this?" I said to Bartholomew.

"Nothing, alright?" said Bartholomew.

"Speak, man!" And Bartholomew, much disconcerted, unfolded all he knew, namely that John had sold his rights to this fellow, Paul, who supplying John with copious notes, sought to make this story of the rebel Jew into a modern-day blockbuster.

"Twists and exaggerates he does. Why changes the very meaning," said Bartholomew.

"Yes, inevitably," I said, "for mankind lacks discernment. That's his destiny. If not this Paul, then another. And yet I'll go visit the man and explain a thing or two."

"Hallo, editor!" I called out in my customary manner. *Paul* was reading a manuscript in a distracted way whilst totting up numbers on an adding machine and talking on the telephone.

"Greatest story ever told, I'm telling you," he said.

I sauntered over to his desk and pressed the hook switch, disconnecting the call.

"Hello! Hey! You can't just come in here hanging up telephones!"

"No?"

"How'd you like it?"

"Woulds't not."

"So there!"

"Okay now?"

"Sure, sure. No big deal. He called me. What do you want?"

"I'm here about that thing you're working on with John."

"John … John. Don't know a John."

"Everyone knows a John."

"No…."

"Big bumptious fellow? Calls himself a disciple?"

"Oh, *that* John!"

"Yes, that."

"Why yes, was telling me a story about this fantastical fellow who goes about healing the lame and curing the blind. Great story. A little slow in parts."

"Wait till you get to the end."

"How's that?"

"The end."

"Know you the end?"

"Of course."

"But how?"

"Knowest the story."

"But how?"

"Why am a-telling it now…. You're in it too."

"Fascinating. Have I a say? How's it turn out?"

"A great deal more to say than I'd like. How it turns out I'll tell you."

"Myself, I mean. How do I turn out?"

"Somewhat decapitated, I'm afraid."

"Oh no! Cans't change?"

"Cannot change a word, for 'tis no fiction, man; 'Tis happening as we speak. This fellow to whom you refer, who goes about healing the lame and the blind, were no character in a Cheever story; why 'tis Jesus Christ of Nazareth, a historical personage. The tale *you* tell plays fast and loose with facts."

"Well, sometimes that can't be helped, I'm afraid."

"Aye, and sometimes would reveal a deeper truth; yet these Judeans are literal-minded folk and understand only what's in front of their face. The esoteric meaning's lost on them."

"As you say."

"Would aggrieve me if I had any real business in this realm. As I am from another, can only lament the loss. Look you then after some semblance of fact. Not so much with the miraculous nonsense. Leave metaphysics out of it. I tell you this not as a friend; yet shall my enmity elevate you to the rank of a saint, G-d only knows why."

"A saint you say!"

"I'm not getting through to you, am I? Wouldst like a little demonstration?" And here I produced a bit of devilry; showed this Paul to himself in various iterations, one a-swatting a shuttlecock in pristine whites upon some heavenly playing field, another licking festering flanks, dog-like, in hell.

"Get me? Paul? … Look you not after false treasure or what glitters, for this world is built upon a bedrock of truth despite much dissembling, above as below; a truth, aye, that supports such notions as man may dream, as steel girds a façade. Tell it thou wilt or swear I shall hunt thee down, in heaven or in hell. Get you my meaning, Paul?"

"Who *are* you?"

"Ah, the Devil knows."

Thus a Pawn Becomes a Queen

Indeed, what the Devil *knows* would fill many pages.— Why, jumped upon a crocodile once. Counted the rings of Saturn. Weighed a tear. (Yet here would man march obediently to the altar on Sunday and stick out his tongue to receive mysteries!)

(Well. 'Tis not my story….)

And what G-d said back at Al Maghtas? I won't tell. Better you should guess for yourselves. Yet I'll give you the gist: "Stay close." Thus G-d wiping his hands clean drifted back up to heaven, leaving the Devil to sort His mess.— I say *His mess* by the same logic He would say *His divine plan, His creation, His Dog-rose* … for if the Devil's G-d's, then the Devil's G-d's.

How often I replayed this match, exchanging pawn for pawn, knight for knight, so to speak, defending, attacking, hording my pieces here, sacrificing there, yet saw each time I peered down the files only crushing defeat.

Perhaps there's a kind of comfort in that; indeed, it's how the Devil sleeps at night.— Yet on this night 'twere no sleep.

I wandered the synagogue listening to the disciples muttering to themselves from the depths of their dreams.

"Give here!" called John aloud.

"No, no!" murmured Peter, as if in reply.

A single star burned in the gap of the synagogue's roof beams.

So this was it, I thought to myself, regarding the disciples sprawled in the dirt: man's crowning achievement.— *Aye, like the head of an infant crowning from its mother's vagina,* I chortled to myself.

Someone broke wind loudly.

"Who's there?" shouted Thomas.

"Shut the fuck up; go back to sleep." I kicked Thomas in the ribs.

"Peace, Beelzebub," came a voice out of the darkness.

I started a little guiltily.

Jesus sat in a corner illuminated by ambient light coming through the roof.

"Look here," he said: a chess board gouged into the dirt and 32 little pieces fashioned from twisted wheat heads.

"Play?"

Yes, inevitably, I thought.

Jesus held out his hands and I chose a gold-yellow pawn. Jesus opened his other hand revealing a piece dyed rust-brown, like blood.

We arranged the board and I opened with the king's pawn.

Jesus' hand hovered above the queen's bishop, and he looked archly up at me, then simply pushed his king's pawn.

I brought out my knight.

Then he brought out that bishop's pawn.

I didn't like that little outpost he'd set up, the dis-equilibrium, so moved the queen's pawn, *en passant,* which he took, and I took back with my knight, feeling a little foolish of a sudden with my knight sitting exposed in the middle of the board like that, an apt metaphor for the Devil's nature— rash, sanguinary—and pushed a pawn to protect. Next move he attacked with his bishop, and seizing the tempo kept after me, harassing this position I'd foolishly staked out.

At length I managed to shift the fight to the king's side of the board, yet as I pressed the attack he began to push a single pawn down the vacated queen's. As I had more pressing matters I let it go, but kept an eye out; yet each time he attacked, simultaneously covered the pawn's advance.

We'd reached a certain point late in our mid game and I looked up from the board disoriented, you know, and glanced about at the humped figures of the disciples. It was all quiet now; even the crickets and the katydids had quit their racket, and the night seemed to deepen a final shade.

Jesus checked with his queen. I took with my rook, leaving the last rank undefended, and Jesus moved that wayward pawn to the promotion square, putting me in check.

"Thus a pawn becomes a queen," I said.

"And a queen is resurrected, " Jesus said.

And looking more closely I saw that he'd forked the rook.

"Son of a bitch."

I let it lay there and went off to bed.

"Shall finish this," I said.

In the morning John and Peter were playing checkers, but I'd memorized the board and considered my next move the day long.

At last that evening, the disciples abed, I dragged the board back out.

"Shall finish?"

"Aye," Jesus said.

And we settled down, two old friends late in the night, in the corner of the room, with a bottle of wine between us.

I moved my king out of check, and Jesus ignoring the rook, brought his own king out.

I considered briefly, then again at length. It made no sense. So moved the rook.

Jesus moved the king again.

Well, if there were some deeper plot, I failed to see it.

The game continued in this way. Each move Jesus made was more incomprehensible than the last. Yet he covered his pieces; indeed, played all the more brilliantly to mitigate each blunder.

At last all of our pieces were arrayed in the center of the board as if in some final confrontation.

Here I played with great cunning, isolating one piece, then another, until at last I had surrounded the king. A lone, desultory knight sat off by itself, so there was no danger of forcing a stalemate. And I saw mate in two moves.

Jesus moved the knight aimlessly. He must have seen what I saw, yet would not resign.

"Say, what are you playing at, Jesus?" I said.

"The game."

"What game?"

"Why this one."

"And yet it seems you play another."

"A game within a game. How novel."

"Mock me?"

"No, Beelzebub. The game. This game, bounded on all sides by a board. A game of infinite possibilities, yet one outcome, or two."

"Or draw…."

"You think He'd allow that!"

"No."

"And so play, merely, by His rules. And yet my own game, by my own logic."

"Were that possible."

"'Tis. Watch me," Jesus said. "Your move."

Barabbas

Now were joined on occasion by various travelers who stayed a night or a week at Capernaum and then left fulfilled or unfulfilled. Disillusion was not uncommon, but the disciples' faith was firm and those who left were soon forgotten.

By and by a group of four men, a Barabbas and an Abbas and two others of no account, came to visit, whom Jesus extended every courtesy, as was our custom, hoping he might assimilate them into the life of the synagogue.

This Barabbas was an unregenerate fellow who made not the slightest pretense of getting with the program. Whilst he lounged about clipping his toenails, his understudy, Abbas, poked into all the corners of synagogue, looking for something of worth; the other two, meanwhile, seemed content eating their share, pissing themselves and bumming smokes—a particular grievance of my own.

When we went out to gather grains they made excuses. "Have toothache something awful," Barabbas said. And when fishing complained of seasickness. All this Jesus forbore, while the apostles grew restless.

"'Shall bring us ill-repute," complained John.

"Are so worried about your reputation, John?" said Jesus, laughing.

"Well, yes, in fact," said John.

"My blanket's gone missing," joined Peter.

"We'll get you another blanket, Peter."

"Carries with him a knife," said Bartholomew."

"So carries a knife," said Jesus.

"A man carries only what he will use," said Bartholomew.

—And here I guiltily fingered the thing I kept in my pocket; kept it there because I liked the feel of it; kept, too, for sentimental reasons. Had traded it for open G.— No great discovery, really, was just a-lying there.— Fingered the cool hardness of it, thinking there might be something in what Bartholomew said about a man carrying only what he will use....

The next morning, as we were headed out, Jesus accosted these hangers-on. "Shall join us today? There's berries ripening on the field."

"Not today," said Barabbas. "I have to meet a man."

"Perhaps after."

"No, shall be occupied."

"I think," said Jesus, "you might lend an effort to our efforts."

"Don't worry, brother, the Lord shall provide," said Barabbas.

And the day long, as we reaped in the field, Jesus seemed to struggle with a question.

That night, as we ate our fill of bread and jam, the four hung about the table making pitiful faces.

"Brother, spare us some bread," spake Abbas.

"Hath not the Lord made provisions?" said Jesus.

"Have not a-seen today," said Barabbas.

"Hath not gone out a-looking?" said Jesus.

"Had other business," said Barabbas.

"Poor business, indeed," said Jesus, "that leaves one a-begging."

And Barabbas withdrew into the shadows making a horrible face.

Later that night there was a disturbance as we slept, and Barbara could be heard speaking to Jesus in urgent undertones.

The next day the apostles accosted Jesus.

"Shall not have them," said john.

"Whose place to say what shall and shall not have?" spake the Lord in anger. "Whose place to reject what God hath ordained?"

The disciples hung their heads, knowing the truth of Jesus' saying, yet firm in their own knowledge of the street. There was nothing to be gained by the presence of these interlopers, and everything to be lost. Surely, Jesus saw this too; but he seemed constrained by any appearance of hypocrisy.

Now Bartholomew, who spoke little, but spoke to the point, said aloud, "We had an old saying back on the strand, a bit of a cliché I'm afraid, that when you give a man a fish he eats for a day; but teach a man to fish…."

And Jesus smiled upon this Bartholomew whom he had come to rely upon for his thoughtful nature. "I think you may have something there, Bartholomew."

And they prevailed upon Barabbas and his compatriots to accompany them to the lake. On the way down the four dragged their feet, looking for one pretext or another to forestall whatever was in store.

"I forgot my sandals," said Barabbas.

"Shall not need," said John.

"My blanket," said Abbas.

"Shall keep it company for thee, said Peter, taking Abbas by the scruff of his neck as the disciples crowded in amongst the four men, shepherding them down the hill.

"But what's this?" complained Barabbas.

"A lesson in self-reliance," said Jesus gleefully.

"Shall not come with?" asked Barabbas.

"Aye, shall be with thee anon," said Jesus.

And the disciples took an old beater and sat the four upon its thwarts.

A steady wind blew down from the hills as Jesus waded into the water, pointing the boat downstream. "Shall find fish just out there," Jesus said.

"Now hold fast to this rope and don't let go," he said as the little boat lurched forward.

The four of them looked back at us, affrighted, as they struggled with the rigging, which they had no proper knowledge of. And as they ran down the lake, the boom whipped back and forth, bumping them upon the heads. At length they lost the sheet, and the sail flapped uselessly before them. And as the current took the little boat down the coast, we suppressed great bursts of laughter.

"Shall fetch up at Tiberius, right?" said Jesus.

Blood Oath

Now the time had come for Jesus to speak plainly. "Soon, brothers, we shall be put to the test. Whilst we go about feeding the poor and mending barns, there are those who regard our efforts as an affront to their own. I speak of Jerusalem and of Rome."

The apostles nodded to a man, no strangers to the petty vindictiveness astride them—the revocation of a license, the arbitrary levy of a tax, to which they had all been subjected at one time or another.

Jesus continued: "And while it is a simple matter to rebel against authority, it is another to stand accused."

"But have committed no crime," said Peter.

"All the more hateful in the eyes of the law," said Jesus, "which sees only guilt; yea, and finding none, finds the worse." Jesus paused here to let his meaning sink in. "Why, this utterance alone were enough to incite the state, the very thought an act of sedition."

The apostles stirred uneasily as if trying to shift the meaning of Jesus' words.

"Think not, oh you disciples, that we labor only for the welfare of Judea; our mission extends to all mankind.— Nor that we live for this moment alone; our labor is in the field of time."

The screeching of barn swallows pierced the evening air as they darted about the synagogue after insects flying out of the grass.

"The time has come to break ties," said Jesus, "for down shall we go into the dirt and the loam of life, where live roots suck at life-giving mineral— only for dilettantes to gaze at flowers, mere ornaments—no, down into the decaying calculus of empire, the very compost of ourselves, shall we a-go, like those same roots that heave at foundations and topple stones in the sun. In suffering injustice shall we reform the law. In showing man his darkness shall we turn him toward the light … Last, ye disciples, know this for certain—and here is my point—that the least thing done unto me, shall be done unto thee. Let any man who is opposed slip away now."

The disciples were quiet for many minutes, their expressionless faces like many ripe fruits hung along a bough.…

How well I knew this moment of reckoning, rather the inverse of my own dealings, yet bargain all the same, when one hands over a pen dipped in blood.

Gangsters know this. Clergy, too. Lacking legal means or the bonds of family, they bind with mysterious rites, with blood and with promises. Jesus was neither of these things, of course, yet aware that he pulled his disciples into this vortex, offered them a choice: relinquish this life and live in G-d's everlasting glory … or what? Walk away? Disappear? Dwell eternally in the ignominy of a wasted life? Was that not the tacit understanding? Wasn't it? Or am I mistaken? Did Jesus not burden his disciples with the same fate assigned to him? That same fate he rejected … and yet without the where-withal to reject, for these apostles were earnest fel-lows? It was this point, precisely, that I'd railed against. And the thought of it chafed like a nail sticking through a shoe.

"You know me," said John at last.

"Aye," said Phillip.

"And you, Bartholomew, I'd like to know what you have to say."

"I had hoped," Bartholomew said with a sigh, "despite my humble beginnings, to study the law one day and to enter into conversation with those great minds; God willing, to make my own mark; yet I plainly see great cause in this convocation."

And one by one, the disciples gave their assent. Then Jesus took a dagger from a niche inside the wall and drew it across his hand.

"This is my blood," said Jesus, "which I shed for you and for all men so that sins may be forgiven. This is the blood of the new and everlasting cov-enant. Whoever does so shall be with me forever and ever. Amen."

And one by one, now, the disciples came for-ward with hand outstretched to mingle their blood with the blood of the Lord, who drew the dagger across their flesh and pressed his palm into theirs: Bartholomew, John, Thomas, yet when he came to Peter drew the blade so that it pierced not the flesh.

The Wedding at Cana

Such is time that it accelerates toward its destined object whilst we blindly grope in some bootless present moment. Jesus, sensing the whirlwind of events all around him, tried to match that speed. Here we spent the day at a local orphanage, there fetched bodies from a shipwreck, there subdued a madman and returned him to his parents. No doubt Jesus and his disciples materially benefitted the lives of those Judeans, yet for every calamity we attended, two more cropped up. All the while, time slipped away.

"Would stay and do this work," Jesus said, pulling me aside, "as futile as our efforts seem in the face of so much suffering, for 'tis the work alone that counts, I'm sure of it. It grieves me, therefore, that I've been chosen for something so symbolic…."

Jesus sat on his haunches, and reaching for an ironwood twig began to doodle distractedly in the dust.

"In fact, I'm wary of the very thing," I said, squatting next to him and looking into his face. "For the sooner one lifts one's head to search about for a meaning, the sooner meaning's lost…. Yet will your example inspire many."

"Do you really think so?"

"The long answer? Obviously I've no real soft spot in my heart for man. In truth am indifferent. And if I'm fearsome in my role as a punisher of human sin, it's only my distaste for the job … indeed, a distaste for hypocrisy, cowardice, ugliness and all those other human emotions that attend damnation. Would spend my time scanning sonnets, you know…. And yet I admit, Thou hast shown me something of the dignity in human suffering. Shall remember Syrus and those others, particularly. Have shown me, perhaps, that in dignity lies a kind of freedom...."

Jesus reached out with his hand and cupped my neck in his manner, and his body was racked with sobbing.

"But let us attend happier occasions, where there is yet work to do," Jesus said, collecting himself. "Fetch me my disciples and bid them trim their beards and put something decent on."

There was a wedding at Cana that we decided to crash, so we loaded the mules with plenty of wine and dates and some goat meat, knowing that these country affairs tended to be poorly provided for.

Along the way, Barbara told her story.

"Tell us about your marriage," said Peter.

"Mine? Oh, it's a common story, I'm afraid."

"No, tell us," the apostles said.

Barbara began reluctantly. "At first there was a lot of passion, which I thought would mature into love, but never did. When we were first married, you know, he used to bring me a little bouquet of cowslip. Would a-lie next to me in the morning stroking my cheek. Within a year he was out with his mates, you know how that goes, and in the morning lay abed moaning whilst I tended to the chores."

"At first I took it for evidence of character, of some inner torment or poetic nature. Within a year he merely smelt. My own mother counseled patience, but when I looked to her marriage, I wondered what price, patience.

"Worse, would come home drunk demanding favors, which I obliged….

"At last I moved his trophy shelf from the corner of the house to make room for a crib. He'd come home drunk again and demanded to know where his things were, accusing me of disloyalty, saying I only wanted to tear him down. And then he raised his hand to me. Well, after that I sought out an apothecary…. There, how's that? Not very inspirational, sorry.

"I'm sorry," Peter said, putting his arm about her shoulder. "You're one of us now."

"Don't be sorry, Peter. I'd have made him a wife if he hadn't broken his vow, it's true, for saw nothing disagreeable in it; yet had no other recourse open to me. Had I known then that a woman might make her own way in this world, why might have chosen differently. Such choice, why the very idea, still seems incredible.

" … A very silly boy," she added as an after-thought. "Why once a-sent him to market for eggs and returned with hair gel," she said, suppressing a sob.

As expected, the wedding party was a modest affair. A homely bride sat next to an emaciated young man with bulging eyes while the guests milled tentatively in small groups, wondering if they might get a bite to eat.

The bride rose to greet us when we came through the front door, and the groom brought a little cup of water with a thimble of wine. Jesus, much moved, took a gold ring he wore and placed it upon the bride's finger, and he embraced the groom and whispered into his ear. Then he shouted to the apostles to make ready. There was a rush of activity as meat was roasted and copious amounts of wine poured into the little stone cistern in the yard and music played by some musicians we'd picked up along the way.

There was rejoicing and feasting, and many old and haggard people approached Jesus to thank him;

and in the young, who frolicked happily about, one could not help but see dim futures. Handsome boys and lissome girls with all their hopes and dreams dancing before them, in a mere decade would be their parents…. And perhaps sensing the narrowness and the futility of these lives, Jesus began to speak from the depths of his heart.

"Let us rejoice in the love between a man and a woman: this Abel and this Sarah," Jesus said, and the crowd hushed—except for someone talking volubly in the corner. "Let us rejoice, *John,* in what is simple and plain," Jesus said pointedly. "I know you have much to say. And there will be time to speak of water and wine, and of wine and other things to come. But we are here, now, in this holy place—and in looking elsewhere we lose sight of what is good and sufficient in ourselves; then all is truly lost. Therefore, let no man impute to greater or lesser cause that which resides in his own heart. Know that what is true for thee is true for all mankind. And what is true for all mankind is true for God. Yet keep thy counsel. Eat, drink, love. In tending that love you will find what is required of you. Amen." And all around the people embraced and celebrated their good fortune.

The bride, whose one leg was shorter than the other, seemed to hide in the shadows. Then Barbara was seen talking with her and pinching her cheek and leading her out to the dance floor where she ambled about with her groom.

Then her next sister, since both the parents were dead, made a toast: "My sister, Sarah, how will we manage our house without thee, who fed us and clothed us and raised us up from our situation? Yet while there are a few years left, raise thine own family, remembering me and our poor father and mother and little Jacob and Sarai," and overcome by emotion she clung to her chair.

An elderly aunt came to her side and overcome herself, led the poor girl back to the family, a collection of old women and children for the most part, the men all since passed away from hardships or fled to greener prospects.

I was out back taking a piss when Jesus came up next to me.

"Water into wine, wine into water. What's the diff?" he said.

"Huh?"

"John."

"Oh. Some mouth on that one, though."

"Of all the men that I've gathered about me and all those yet to come, that one worries me most."

"All part of the plan, right?"

"And yet one almost wishes it could have been otherwise...."

Jesus Lays Hands
on the Faithful

Many strangers were seen in Capernaum in the following weeks. Word traveled of this Jesus and of his works, some called them "miracles."— It is a peculiarity of human nature, my friend, to believe in miracles; a defect in man's soul that compels him to go searching for answers behind locked doors…. Yes, I spent an afternoon as a boy trying to shift a penny with my mind. Then it occurred to me that were such a thing possible—by some sort of alchemy or other—it wouldn't really be any miracle after all, and I gave the thing up as unworthy of my time. Yet humanity—*humans*—with their very finite existence, go on speculating about one world hidden behind another as if the very mystery of their mortal existence weren't enough to occupy their thoughts— the evidence of the senses insufficiently real….

Such miracle seekers were to be found in Capernaum. By and by they came sniffing around the little synagogue, if only for a thrill. (I was on the lookout for one who was not Judean. I knew he was on his way. He was near now.)

Jesus sat against the wall, eyes closed, head back. It seemed he had the spirit of the lion upon him now, content to wait out the heat of day until evening lit a spark in his brain. The apostles sat quietly at his feet. Onlookers murmured in the background.

Jesus opened his eyes and looked about him for long moments, musing, I suppose, on his recent reversal of fortune and the new role thrust upon him. The Jesus I knew was a man galvanized by events, a man whose philosophy was born of *praxis*. He hated didacticism, institutional authority, orthodoxy. He disliked to be pinned down…. He searched the ground now as if looking for an object that might serve as a metaphor for what was in his mind.

Sunlight filtered through the roof. The light swam with dust motes. Jesus smiled knowingly, as if some distant, ethereal thought had settled into his brain.

"What is the object of man's striving?" Jesus said. "Is it to be a citizen? A son? A father? A Jew?" he asked rhetorically. "To be rich? To be famous? To be admired among men? Or is it to be first a man? … Of course it is to be first a man, for a man can be no other thing than himself, nor to himself— nor any other thing until he is first a man! For what is a man but that which is in his nature? Verily, he can be no other thing until he is first himself. Let the angels sport in angelic fashion. Let the gods dispose as they see fit. And let man contend with what is mortal. That is his fate, and a glorious fate it is to struggle … " Jesus paused, and looked aside, and he spoke inwardly, thus:

Aye, to struggle beyond all futility, as the dust struggles to remake itself a stone and a stone struggles to rebuild a temple; and the temple to redeem a people…. Yea, God hath designed well, making man of more perishable stuff.

And he looked up at the crowd again and began speaking in little more than a whisper, his voice rising with emotion:

" … Thus I leave it to you to find out what is truly in your nature … not as has been taught thee, but what thou art, man, in thy brains and in thy sinews, and who and what thou mayest become.… *Arise!* I say, for this bold experiment may be gone in a twinkling of an eye and naught remain but footprints in the sand.… Rise above!" Jesus stood and hauled a disciple up by the collar, "Rise above," he hollered, punching another man in the chest. "Rise above," he spun about and glared at me, "Rise above!" he shouted, elbowing his way into the crowd.

And one by one, people began to jostle each other, hungry for contact with the energy that came off of Jesus; hungry, too, for the energy that came off of themselves.

Then I saw him in the corner, motionless, as all the others gyrated. He saw me, too, and for a moment our eyes locked. And a disgust welled up in me—for him as well as myself—and sensing this he disappeared in the crowd.

"Rise above!" the crowd chanted.

Jesus Lays Hands on the Faithful

People were jammed in the doorway now, surging around Jesus, who turned like an axis with arms outstretched. Then a beam of light descended from the roof as a cripple was lowered by ropes into the outstretched hands of the crowd. "Rise above!" they shouted as they bore the cripple along. "Rise above!"

Jesus turned and the crowd turned, circling him like bees around a hive a full five-hundred and twelve times, mad for their queen. Then all at once Jesus stopped and walked to a corner of the room where the stranger stood half in shadow.

"Welcome brother," Jesus said, and kissed the man on the cheek.

"Good Shabbos," said the stranger.

"Shabbat shalom," replied Jesus. "What do you call yourself?"

"Judas Iscariot," the stranger said.

"Yes, we've been expecting you," Jesus said.

Judas

Now this Judas was cut from a different cloth, so to speak, a cosmopolitan and sophisticate. His clothes, in fact, were of a different cloth and cut, and he wore them with an insouciance that I found not altogether unflattering. Clearly he flattered himself. And he approached me talking with that practiced, lawyerly speech.

"Beelzebub, yes? Judas. Iscariot."

"I know."

"Have we met?

"I don't think so."

"Damascus? Giza?"

"Possibly."

"Small world," he said looking about him … "Some outfit, this, though."

"We like it."

"I've heard things. Wondrous strange…."

"I'll bet."

"… and thought I might be of service somehow."

A waiter brought two añejos. I stared into the amber liquid inside the glass, considering the mysteries therein; drank and stiffened. The drink touched something low and mean inside me, and I took the gun out of my waist, flipped it open, sited the rounds and snapped it shut again. Then I put the gun on the table between us and looked into the eyes of this Judas Iscariot, who recovering himself quickly stared back at me. And G-ddamn if I didn't see myself.

"You seem to have come in at the end, Judas Iscariot."

"Is that right?"

"Yeah."

"You have a proposition?"

"I have a proposition. More like an ultimatum. You know the saying, I'm sure. *Plomo o plata.*"

"I heard it in the movies."

"And so it is; we're in this beautiful movie. Love and death, and the hero can't help himself."

"I take it we help him."

"I take it *you* help him."

"Okay…."

"Sure you don't want to think it over any?"

"No, I'm okay."

—Just like that. *I'm okay,* he said. No conscience to speak of. Neither delight nor disgust in the act. A truly modern man, equal to the amorality of his age.

One might have wondered at length at this Judas had not one more pressing engagements, yet I considered him for a moment as he perched on his barstool watching cursive loops of cigarette smoke.

What possible stake did he have in this business? None that I could see. Call him a mistake of nature, a cancer cell bent on destroying the host for his own short-term gain. A pinworm. A virus. Yet not a mistake, for nature does not make mistakes— or if so, absorbs them. Either way, he was part of the pattern and plan. Here I paused, not so much struck by the old theodicy question of one's school days as transfixed by G-d's dark vision.

This Judas had been sent straight from G-d with a bomb strapped to his chest on a veritable suicide mission.— Oh, tell me not *In order to bring about G-d's greater glory*. If so, then G-d's a terrorist. Nor to punish man, nor reward him with free-will. What, then? Merely to amend a mistake. This G-d, who had lost man to man's desire for knowledge, would make a mockery of that knowledge, confuse, confound and dissemble: *Here, I give you my only son. Kill him. I forgive you. I'm a mystery.* (Woof.)

… And Jesus, walking a tightrope, who would only preach love and forbearance:

"Yea, I have overcome the world."

And God: "So sit at God's right hand."

Jesus: "So make a channel of peace."

"To live in God's everlasting love."

"To love my neighbor as myself."

"And thus enter the kingdom."

"'Tis here."

"Where?"

"In me."

"And yet perish. Then nowhere."

"Why, 'tis all about us, in the least flower and greatest whale."

Now the days became an endless round of running from town to town. Each place another crowd awaited Jesus. The blind, the lame, the poor; lepers, whores; the abused in spirit, broken in flesh and weak in mind all shoved their way toward him, clutching at his sleeves and imploring him: "Jesus heal me." "Touch me Lord." "Have mercy Savior." I mean, *really*…. Mind you, Jesus never did aught to encourage or discourage them, one way or another. He merely listened whilst they poured the flames of their torment upon him. Yet that alone seemed to satisfy them. And they believed themselves healed.

Now there was a family known to one of the apostles whose father lay dying of tuberculosis. Wherever we went a messenger inveigled Jesus to come heal the man. The apostles, too, had begun to lobby Jesus: *Why couldn't he save this Lazarus?*— for it seemed that credulity had afflicted even those closest to Jesus, who should have known better. And the apostles contrived, at last, to take Jesus up to this man's house.

As we approached, a distinct keening could be heard, and it became clear that this Lazarus had died and the family was in full mourning. His sons tore at their clothes and the man's daughters ran barefoot across the rocky slope bruising their heels as they went.

"Why didn't you come?" "Why have you left our poor father to die?" they said, reprimanding Jesus.

"Bring me to Lazarus," Jesus said. And they led us to a sepulcher, in truth a hole in the ground, where the corpse lay covered with loose gravel, and Jesus bid them uncover it.

As the body was brought up, Jesus peeled back the winding sheet. Lazarus grimaced. One blue eye stared out of its socket as if fixed upon a distant image ... but death was upon the other side of the face. The eye was sunk into the head and the living shape gone out of the flesh.

The apostles, who had gathered eagerly about the grave, took a step back and made superstitious gestures, biting at the flesh of their palms and so forth.

Jesus checked them with a look. For long moments he caressed the dead man's head, *thinking hard for all of us.* Then he stood and rolled the body back into its grave.

"Your husband is dead," Jesus said to the grieving widow. "Gather your family about you and order your house. Set your sons to whatever tasks as they are wont and find families for the girls. As for you, sister, take solace in the love that you shared with your husband and the years which, though they seem to vanish, abide...."

And Jesus kissed the woman on both cheeks, and he lay his forehead upon the foreheads of Lazarus' daughters and embraced his sons. "God's will be done."

It was a desultory trip back to Capernaum. The apostles straggled behind, talking amongst themselves, and at a turning in the road there was a commotion. John and Judas had come to blows.

"And who are you?" John screeched.

Jesus interceded and led us to some shade under an olive tree.

"Avast, ye fishermen! You'll drown us for sure before we've had sight of land. Look you now John and you Judas: I've recruited each of you to play his own part. Stick to the script, in short...."

"Know that Lazarus' sons have lost a father. Know too that Lazarus lost a father, and his father a father…. What would you have me say that the poets haven't already said—or will say? Or *do?*" And Jesus, who despite contemporary accounts of himself as some great sermonizer, who indeed suspected words altogether as falsifiers of original human feeling, struggled to compose his thoughts. At length words came to him, and he spoke sternly as one speaks to a child.

"Fear not death, for death will come as surely as morning follows night and night follows the day. But look on death as one waking from a troubled sleep who finds himself untroubled upon waking. Yet forget not the sleep to come.

"Neither glorify death nor despise it, but regard it as one regards the tides that break ceaselessly upon the shore. Understand that death has been with thee all thy living days, entwined with thy very life as two serpents coiled. Meditate, then, on that mystery if thou art strong.

"Otherwise, look to good deeds. Perhaps your efforts will bear fruit for some future generation.— And what *of* those future generations? Will they not have their own tribulations? Yea, I say unto thee, each man and each woman must endure their own trial, for all shall pass the way of the earth.

"As thy last deed, then, separate thyself from the joys and the sorrows of this life gracefully. If you cannot reconcile yourself with God, reconcile yourself with nature, of which thou art part. Whosoever sayeth otherwise is a fraud and a blasphemer.

Thus spoke Jesus Christ, it is true; I heard these words spoken myself and swear to them because they are true and because they are lost. What Jesus taught did not comport with the religion of man, for men, whether they are rigging up a ministry or a crusade, are only concerned with establishing their own authority.— *(Oh, the lies men tell! The Devil lies, knowing he lies. Man lies believing.)*

Now there were those coming up the road making a ruckus. Amidst much shouting and remonstrating they overtook us, bearing aloft an open casket with an effigy of the resurrected corpse of Lazarus. Indeed some of the apostles mixed with the crowd, making inquiries and talking excitedly and behaving as if they believed the thing before them. Then the crowd passed on and the apostles slinked back to Jesus.

They Line the Roads

Word spread of this last, greatest miracle, and a council was set up in Jerusalem to hear charges laid against Jesus. A lot of scribes and pharisees crowded the bar, making their arguments to the high priests.

"They call him King—*King,* mind you," spake a cross-eyed fellow in a yellowed yarmulke. "Setting aside our own authority for the moment, through which we maintain peace amongst our own tribes, consider how it is received in Rome."

"Yes, yes, Rome," the chief priest, Caiaphas, spoke wearily. "And how is it received amongst your own constituency?"

"We've lost the handle, quite frankly," spoke another, pulling thoughtfully at his beard.

"What you're asking, then, is that I should ask Rome to intercede on our behalf."

"… acknowledging our mutual interest," continued the man with the yarmulke.

"Mutual interest? Rome deals with us because we've stepped forward to deal with Rome … who will deal with another just as soon. It's a matter of diplomacy."

"Our point precisely, your honor."

"Yes … And this Jesus?"

"Why a truculent fellow who travels about in a group of fishermen stirring up the popular sentiment—yet attended by one more worrisome than the rest, half a head taller with a penetrating look."

"Why, I know these! A-came to me in my tent whilst I was camped in the wilderness."

"Then you know them?"

"Their likes, indeed."

"With respect, Your Honor, we've *not* seen their likes before," came a voice from the back of the court.

"Who's this?" said Caiaphas. "Show yourself."

An elderly gentleman stepped forward making bland motions. "My concern, your honor, is neither for Rome nor for ourselves, but the very truth...."

"Oh, is *that* all?"

A snickering came from the bench.

"You, must have seen for yourselves, you scribes and pharisees, how each generation hatches plots anew to disrupt the established order. 'Tis the excesses of youth, merely. They feel they've been treated unfairly."

"'Tis more I fear than a hollow pecking inside an egg; the egg they peck at's the world."

"Indeed."

"Right now he has three thousand followers with him, camped along the shores. Where he goes, they go. Last night they overwhelmed a census ... and ran a rabbi out of temple, bound backward upon an ass!"

"Oh, that's not good."

"You may think it a harmless bit of fun out in the countryside; when they come to Jerusalem for Passover you'll think differently."

"Here? Why that messianic schtick won't play here."

"They line the roads right now, waiting for him as we speak."

Wilt Thou?

Jesus rallied those disciples about him, who despite their unquestioning love were filled with a great many questions indeed.

"This is the end," Jesus said.

"Lord?" they said.

"The harvest at long summer's end, when grain is hauled into sheds and fields plowed back under and the boats are laid up high upon the beach."

Such pastoral images seemed to appease these homesick fishermen.

" … Yet there is one who still ventures upon the deep, with iron fingers gripping frozen sheet," Jesus said.

"Yes, Jesus," the disciples said.

"Beyond reef and watery horizon."

"Tell us what to do, Lord!"

"I say to thee, Harrow *thyselves,* fishermen, for thou shallt be called to account, as I shall be called to account, as indeed all shall be called."

"We're with you, Lord."

"Yet must each man be with himself in the end."

"Oh, Lord."

"Yea, comes a time, so soon it comes, with memories yet of childhood green, when thou shalt be pitched back into the furnace and all thy worldly semblance blasted in time's fire. Yet while we still have strength, boys, the field is ours, and this day be remembered for what we did."

"What did we do, Lord?"

"Why, stood for what we are, which is no small thing in this cowed world, neither contributing nor surrendering our genius to the calculations of the crowd. For what we are … what we are, mates, is rightly ours. Feel it not, John? Peter?

"Aye, Lord."

"And yet will become clearer. The object is too close to properly discern. Perhaps on the morn, when we arrive in Jerusalem, you will begin to see and to feel in your own hearts the outline of the thing to come."

Jesus struggled mightily to convey his meaning, which perhaps was still clouded by doubts.

" … And much be made of our toils, which in themselves be common, truthfully—though no less for being common."

"Aye, Jesus."

"Therefore, gird yourselves, you fishermen. Prepare a face. And make Jerusalem feel what we are."

"Yes, Lord!"

"Lord," spake Peter. "There are rumors abroad."

"Yes, Peter. Let them rumor, for we shall present ourselves and dispel all doubt."

"Shall oppose?"

"Nay. Nor surrender, but shall give witness by our presence, in the presence of God."

"But what means this?" said john.

"I know, John, that you are eager to construe events. That is the prerogative of history—in which you may have a hand—but not our concern here, for may no man interpret his own fate; instead, may he strip action of all affect: strike straight, fast, hard, and when the day is done, stand naked before eternity.

"For two years now we have stood for the common man, and what is basic and what is decent, and shall not alter what have said or done…. What say ye, fishermen? Shall we not show them how 'tis done in Galilee? Wilt thou, John? Wilt thou Peter? Wilt Bartholomew?

"Aye, wilt!" the fishermen cheered.

Return of the King

Now we rolled into Jerusalem like they do in the movies, high-stepping in slow motion as Mozart's Requiem poured out of speakers strung along the route. *Victorious.*

Confetti swirled in splintering sunlight as after an explosion, and the crowd lay palm fronds at our feet. None of this begging and dunning that plagued our days and nights back in Galilee, the crowd buoyed us along with glad tidings, rich and poor, beggar and publican alike. Even those sent to spy were caught up in the moment.— Say what you will about the falsity of religion; these were the best moments of our lives. Jesus, too, weighed down by the heavy knowledge of death, smiled beatifically.

—And in the far regions I heard the heavenly host singing Hosannas. And behind them the *basso profundo* of G-d, singing along like a groom in his bathtub. Their intrusion here in this human business set me in a bad mood—this meddling, mothering, G-d and his obsequious ducklings—and I raised a finger behind my ear, saluting them smartly.

A bolt of pain shot through my side. So it's true, I thought: *Satan will not be so easily ignored as that.*

Then Jesus slipped his hand inside mine. "Promise me, Beezy," he said.

I turned and looked at this Jesus who I'd known all along, whom I'd striven with for a year or more and who I considered my brother; this ruffian-Jesus and Jesus-philosopher, shining and suffering and looking at me as earnestly as a lamb.

"I promise you," I said.

As we wound our way through narrowing streets, the crowd was squeezed out, and people went home to prepare their Passover celebrations. Jesus booked a hall for our own supper.

The disciples, rather unaware of the imminent crisis, happily arranged the seder plates: a meager lamb shank, few herbs, mostly matzoh and wine, truth be told. What little money we had left Jesus had given away on our trek to Jerusalem as a valedictory gesture of sorts, lastly setting his own sandals beside a sleeping beggar.

"Happy Pesach," the disciple regaled one another in the hubbub.

"Happy Pesach," Peter said unto Thomas.

"Happy Pesach," said Philip unto Bartholomew as they collided, spilling wine."

"Happy Pesach," said John unto Judas.

"Happy Pesach," Judas replied.

And Jesus, much moved, arranged the disciples at the table for a group photo. "Judas, Peter, John, come sit at my right hand…."

In the ensuing confusion I made my way to the front door and slid the bolt shut; stood in front of the group, fingering the revolver in my waist, my ribs still aching from G-d's rebuke.

How easy it would be to put an end to everything right here; a single bullet enough to bring all

G-d's plans crashing down again. How simple to reaffirm my worthlessness in the eyes of G-d and man. How simple to set it all in motion again. What else was left for me? What enjoyment other than to oppose G-d's will?

And I thought of Jesus' own words: "Foxes have dens, and birds of the sky have nests, but the Son of Man has no place to lay His head." There was truth in that and a kind of rough justice.

Then I thought of the gospel of John: "…who eats my flesh and drinks my blood has eternal life." That was a manifest lie. And a little furious point appeared in my brain. I clicked the safety off the gun and went back and forth with the thing in my mind.

Jesus lit candles. *"Baruch Atah Ado-nai, Elo-heinu Melech Ha-olam, Asher Kid'shanu B'mitzvotav V'tzivanu L'hadlik Ner Shel Yom Tov,"* he said. (Blessed are You, Lord our God, King of the Universe, who has sanctified us with His commandments and commanded us that we kindle the Yom Tov lights.)

And holding the cup of wine in his right hand: *"Baruch Atah Ado-nai Elo-heinu Melech Ha-olam Boreh Pree Ha-ga-fen."*

I hung on each word now, having conceived the idea that if he altered the least syllable I'd do it. I'd do it. If he started in with that transubstantiation nonsense, I'd do it … if only to keep them honest.

Jesus played it straight, echoing the old words, reciting the blessings and prayers, and observing a shibboleth that by its very repetition had become empty of meaning.

At last the apostles sang the traditional songs, and during the singing I motioned Judas aside. Unlocking the door I handed him his silver, and as he slipped out handed him the gun. "You'll need this," I said. And Judas disappeared into the night.

Gethsemane

After seder, Jesus led us through the courtyard into the street. It was so dark you couldn't see your hand in front of your face. The moon had set, and in honor of Passover all the Jews about town had drawn their curtains. (Yet the Angel of Death is faultless.)

We followed one another holding hands and groping along walls, whispering in the dark. Every so often someone tripped over a loose cobblestone, cursing as we apostles fished about our ankles for the fallen man, suppressing our mirth.

These were our last carefree moments. Indeed, as we made our way across a wide, starlit plain and up the slope of Mount Olives, Jesus revealed many sorrowful things.

"I will not be with you much longer," Jesus said to the disciples.

"What do you mean?" they said as one.

"I tell you, I will not be with you much longer. Nay, this very night soldiers shall come and arrest me."

"No, Lord!"

"Yes, Peter. Thus has it been decided from the very beginning."

"I don't understand, Lord."

"Understand, Peter, that these are the very limits of our lives, our fates, beyond which it is impossible to traverse. And yet within those margins may act…."

"Am with thee, Lord."

"I know it Peter. And if you accept me, save yourself. Go, now, over the hills to thine old life, unto thy wife and children, and be happy. It may pass, in later years, when thou hast fulfilled thy worldly obligations and thy family is gathered about thee in thy final hours, that thou hast a story to tell. Remember me."

There was a scuffling, then a sound of stumbling and of sobbing receding into the distance. Then Jesus spoke to the rest.

"Stay here whilst I go on to the garden."

And the disciples, much confused and afraid, huddled together and surrendered themselves to the comfort of sleep.

I followed Jesus at a distance and hid behind a tree. A breeze rustled olive leaves and soon I could make out Jesus' voice whispering in prayer.

"Lord, take this cup from me. If thou art pleased, Lord, take it back, for I want it not."

I moved closer. Jesus' face was covered with sweat. Not sweat merely; pink rivulets ran from the corners of his eyes staining the tunic around his neck.

I turned, averting my eyes, and gazed across the valley below, listening to vacuous sounds building one upon another out of the distance.

In a sense, there was nothing unique about Jesus' agony. How many men and women had I witnessed in my time marching to their dooms? Soldiers dying on the field of battle? The falsely accused languishing in prisons? Mothers clutching dead children to aching breasts? The quiet desperation of one coming from the doctor with the oncology report? And I confess, something very unlike sympathy stirred within my breast—that same darkness that passed over me each time I led someone astray; in human terms, the disgust the torturer must feel for his victim as he begs and pleads, thinking, *Why must you make this difficult? Can't you see there would be more dignity in accepting your fate?*

Below, a light appeared, guttering and going out, then reappeared along a path winding up the hill, and I turned and gathered Jesus.

"Get on your feet."

"Is it time yet?"

"Soon."

"So soon?"

There was a fracas below; then soldiers appeared in the garden, shoving apostles before them. And Judas stepped out of the shadows. "Rabbi!" he said, greeting Jesus with a kiss. Then soldiers lay hold of Jesus and bound his wrists.

Arraignment

"Well, well, well, here we are again," spoke the head priest. Despite the late hour the court was crowded and grew more crowded each minute as scribes and pharisees arrived straight from their Passover tables as word spread of this rebel Jesus' arrest.

"Jesus of Nazareth, is it not?" Caiaphas strutted about, making a show. "What say ye?"

Jesus glowered.

"Woulds't proffer charges, first?" said I.

"Ah, this, Abadon, is it not? What business have ye before this court?"

"As counsel for the accused, your grace."

"Very well … And yet I remember some talk about pre-destination."

"We only wish to avail ourselves of due process; otherwise, I fear I'd be remiss, and likely disbarred."

"You are a wag, sir."

"Say you."

"The charge, sirrah, is sedition against the state."

"What state?"

"Why, the holy Roman one."

"Speak you for Rome?"

"Pro statu."

"Pauper imitatione, I think."

"Regardless…." And here one of the crowd spit in Jesus' face.

"What's this?" I objected.

Another laid into Jesus with a bit of cane.

"Stand back!" I said, wrenching the man's arm, bone and sinew breaking beneath my grasp. The man screamed, and the crowd surged forward.

"Restrain this man! You are in contempt, sir!"

And they led me out of the dock and placed me against a wall. Oh, the violence I might wreak! …

Then I felt the old familiar jolt in the side, and I stood down. "A hell of a court, this!"

Caiaphas stepped forward and examined Jesus directly. "They call you *King*. King of *what*, may I ask?"

"King of pain," Jesus snorted, despite himself.

"King of what?"

"King of the lemmings."

"Pardon?"

"King of Kings, you fucking drab."

Caiaphas struck Jesus on the face. "Now look at what you've made me do," he said, rubbing his fingers. A Roman guard stepped forward and hit Jesus with the butt of his rifle.

Jesus reeled under the blow, but stayed on his feet.

"Now, that's right, let's show the proper respect. I ask you again, Jesus of Nazareth, Of whom are you King?

"You tell me, you know," Jesus said.

The soldier raised the butt of his rifle, but Caiaphas stopped him.

"They call you King of the Jews."

"If you say so."

"Why do they call you thus?"

"They tire of quislings."

Caiaphas looked at the soldier, and the butt of the rifle came down again.

Jesus woke in a cell somewhere across town. The whole side of his face ached and his tongue was swollen to twice its normal size. Roman guards milled in the hall.

"Nice *punim,*" I said.

"Who's there?"

"Down here."

"Where?"

"Here. In the corner."

"What, a rat!"

"You'd like a calico, perhaps?"— A flea bit and I scratched furiously behind an ear.

"Oh, Beezy, this is the last!" Jesus laughed and clutched at his head.

A long moment passed.

"Quiet, what?" I said.

"Yes."

"Be sending someone, I suppose."

"I guess."

"So?"

"What?"

"That's it then, you've nothing more to say?"

"What more would I say?"

"Customarily, something. You're to be taken out and crucified in the morning."

Jesus sighed. "It's funny, the more I say, the less it seems I've said; the less I say, the more they make of it … The absurdity, Beezy. Really. I'm tired."

"Rest up bro."

"What for, and act out their final scene?"

"There's that."

"I'll do it, you know."

"I know."

"Somehow it's the only thing left."

"There you go."

" … To defy their will by submitting to it—let the world run away with itself and the fools right along, who only know what they see; clap hooves on a dog and call it an ass. And yet I never meant … I never wanted to be anything other than myself. It's madness to live any other way. That's all I meant to say. That's it in a nutshell."

"To live is to live in the history of one's time."

"I tried! I tried! … believing in my strength and my youth and all that living-in-the-moment nonsense. But I wasn't fast enough! No sooner did I act than the ramifications outran their cause…. So I'll pursue the ends, merely; anything else would be construed as cowardice."

The crack of a gunshot echoed somewhere in the night.

"There it is."

"I love you, Beezy. I love this world and this desert of dust and salt and sunlight—and lament what little I have accomplished these last years of strife and of friendship…. I knew the touch of a woman, once…."

A jangling of jailer's keys sounded in the hallway then, and the Governor of Judea stepped into the doorway, waving guards away.

Jesus leaned on an elbow.

"No need to get up."

Pontius Pilate was tall and clean-shaven and wore his hair brushed forward in the Roman fashion.

"If you'll pardon the intrusion—I know it's late—I wanted to inform you … there shall be no appeal of your sentence. The popular will has spoken and I, being neither in its favor nor out, shall execute…. And indeed it shall go hard for thee; yet that's no reason we shouldn't be friends."

Jesus sat up, curious at this entreaty.

"Can I get you something? Water? Wine?—nothing? That's well," Pilate said, stepping inside the cell and fiddling with a signet ring whilst marshalling his thoughts.

"When I first came out here I had ideas, perhaps as you have ideas … which I found unuseful in the end, toward the smooth administration of state." Pilate glanced about him. "… And find now I care for nothing."

Jesus smiled.

"Yet I confess to a certain foreboding in this case."

Pilate sat on the floor in front of Jesus, much to his amazement.

"I'm not sure what you want me…." Jesus said.

Pilate held up a hand. "I have sent a thousand men to their deaths—rubber-stamped the orders anyway—and shall have to live with that burden … or not live with it. But I have the feeling that this shall be a stain on my conscience and on my name."

"Yes."

"Indeed, am rather certain of it, yet know not how. Tell me, pray."

"I don't know what's in your mind."

"Indeed. I shall tell thee." Pilate stood and wandered the cell, stopping at the grate which gave onto the night sky. A powdery light shone about his head as on the bust of a coin.

"We find ourselves, you and I, at this historical moment, when everything hangs in the balance. Rome is dying—that's plain—and so this ancient world, which has outlived those ideas on which it was founded. 'Tis no great matter for all that. In fact is a relief. Yet as a man who has lived in his time, I wonder at this future in which shall be no more dynasties, only men, as far as I can tell…."

"Aye, comes the age of man, and so shall man prostrate himself before his own image as before a god, no more free."

"Yes."

"Shall sell himself for a straw."

"Yes."

"And speak all manner of foolishness."

"Yes."

"Had better be governed."

"Yes!"

"Yet woulds't change…."

"Change what?"

"Man's conception of himself."

"Into what?"

"Love."

"Love?"

"Aye. Love. To see through life, and all one's hopes and fears; why to see through love itself, to that existence that holds us in its hands...."

Here Jesus fell deep into thought.

"— Surely, Governor, you did not suppose it was thine own native strength that supported thee in thy task."

Pilate nodded a long moment, considering Jesus' words. "Aesthetics, merely, and somewhat sentimental."

"By what other rod measure this world?"

"Truth."

"Truth?" Jesus laughed. "What's that?"

"Ask you me?"

"Aye, for have not seen."

"Why *truth:* What is and what shall be. Indeed, that which prevaileth and is apparent."

"Methinks you confuse truth with power."

"He who has power determines the truth."

"Who has truth has power."

"Think Plato found truth in a cup?"

"As Jesus upon a rood," said Jesus, his head nodding heavily upon his chest.

Many minutes passed. Then Jesus started awake.

"Once I dreamed this world. And awoke in my mother's arms, wise. Spare me, father, or spare me not. Let thy judgement fall as petals plucked from a flower. I care not."

Pilate looked at Jesus with an expression of alarm, then returned to his official self.

"Alas, they shall have sport with thee," spoke Pilate with finality. His eyes glistened in the dark cell. "And though I grieve it, if it's sport they want, then sport shall I give them…. Gall the guards if you can; it may be that one of them strikes a mortal blow, or wounds thee so thy death is swift. *Bene mori.*"

As Pilate's footsteps died down the tunnel a couple of drunken guards entered the cell, fumbling something between them, and grinning, held out a crown of thorns.

Jesus' Son

Dazed from a blow, Jesus lurched out of the prison gate like a bull entering the ring. And a cry went up from the crowd. Though battered and bruised, a bloody crown hammered into his skull—you know the popular image—he yet radiated that strength of his.

Soldiers hauled a rough-hewn wooden cross and sat it upon his back. Jesus staggered under the mass of it, grappled for a moment with the unwieldy dimensions, then taking the cross' measure, hoisted it over his head like a weightlifter, turning for all to see.

Eager to restore the solemnity of the occasion, a soldier hit him in the ribs with his rifle, and the whole *ménage* came crashing down in a heap.

Jesus stood, brushing a sleeve, and wagged a finger at the soldier. There was sporadic tittering in the crowd.

The soldier motioned to the cross.

Jesus motioned to the cross.

More tittering.

As the soldier struggled to help Jesus lift the cross, Jesus slipped from beneath it and placed it upon the soldier.

Great gusts of laughter.

Then a fellow with a bullwhip cut a gash across Jesus' back.

Jesus turned and glared at him, then he shouldered the cross, and the crowd of onlookers, themselves chastened, grew quiet.

An anguished cry rose out of the silence like the cry of birth pains, and Jesus, the cross's crook biting properly into his neck now, began the long slog toward Golgotha.

*

Many terrifying faces lined the route. A gauntlet of human emotions pressed in upon Jesus: faces laughing and crying, jeering and jesting…. These, as much as any cross, seemed to weigh upon Jesus, who despite his infamy could only see himself in simple terms: a carpenter, a Jew—a malcontent, yes, but on his own terms. That his experience bore any relevance to the lives of those around him … that he might provoke the crowd to these lengths, seemed silly. His sudden apotheosis mystified him.

—What form might this Jesus have taken in another incarnation? Many easy answers spring to mind: Buddha, Joan of Arc, Gandhi. None of them quite fit, however, or rather fit so neatly as to reduce Jesus to a type.

Of course it's a hard question when you've literally known *everyone:* Lenny, Lou, Miles—and every other front man who ever actually wanted to *be* Jesus Christ. The Jesus *I* knew shunned the limelight. The Jesus I knew kept time while all those around him were losing their heads, a drummer and garage mechanic. The straight man. A union organizer, maybe. Nothing more than that. And yet fate somehow had decreed that this Jesus of Nazareth might be nailed upon a cross in order to redeem humanity.

"Oh, thou art a wicked generation," Jesus spoke theatrically, and he glanced at me following in the crowd.

The noon day sun beat down unmercifully. Not the least, slender shade fell anywhere, and Jesus moved with difficulty in the damp tunic. Each time he paused to arrange himself, a soldier prodded him from behind.

Jesus turned to these. "Peace, brother. A little patience. Shall have thee home in time for supper. As for me, shall return in my own good time."

"Okay, okay, move along now," spoke the one good soldier, taking Jesus by the arm, fearful of his colleagues, sneering behind his back.

"Peace be with you brother," whispered Jesus.

Now the path narrowed and the crowd pressed in, mocking Jesus. "Traitor!" "Criminal!" they howled, mocking him the more viciously for the weakness in their own hearts, who had not the courage to step out of line themselves and so hated those who did.

Then a cross-eyed bloke in yellow yarmulke tripped up Jesus, who fell painfully with the cross.

Some of the crowd were delighted; others judged it fairly unsportsmanlike. Jesus rose slowly.

"You suppose that'll get you?" Jesus said.

The man shrugged stupidly.

"Points with the big man? Place in heaven?"

Jesus made a brief feint toward the man, who let out a little cry and threw his arm up in self-defense. Jesus laughed. "You fucking disgust me. The lot of you," he said, sneering. "But just a little. Just a little."

A soldier brought the whip down again, and Jesus turned, shaking his head. The soldier raised his arm once more while two others got busy with their rifle butts, and by the time they were done Jesus looked quite a bit worse for wear.

"Oh, Lord." The good soldier bit his lip and moved helplessly in the background.

"Jesus! Here! Jesus!" came a voice from the crowd. And a handsome woman pushed her way to the fore. No longer a flimsy piece of balsa, Mary Magdalene looked quite the proper Sabra now, all hips and henna. Behind Mary came Barbara leading the little leper's child and carrying in her arms another, whose eyes she shielded from the spectacle. And Jesus, recognizing Mary's voice, got to his feet with a great deal of effort. The disorder in his brain quieted now, and Jesus assumed a kind of dignity. He brushed some dirt off of a soldier's tunic and nodded to the other. Tears filled his eyes as he looked upon Mary, and he made to speak, but no words came.

"Don't," said Mary. And she turned and fetched the child and held it for Jesus to see.

A look of disbelief passed over Jesus' face, then deep contentment. And he reached out and stroked the child's face. Now the soldiers, the crowd, the angels, the Devil and G-d himself all remained in abeyance for these moments, as if by magic.

Then Jesus made a little mark upon the child's forehead, and he likewise to Mary; and though Jesus could no longer speak, his jaw broken in several places, I understood his mind and whispered thus to Mary:

"My peace and my blessings I give you, my wife and my child, who have made me happy beyond all reckoning. This mark protect thee from harm…."

Jesus said more, but I kept the words to myself: "… this mark protect thee from harm," he said, "for innocence has gone out of the world … Whatever His will or His intention, there's no peace in this life."

And I gathered the women and the children unto me and sheltered them from the crowd as the soldiers shoved Jesus forward.

Golgotha loomed in the middle distance now like the humped back of some leviathan. Smoke rose and pennants rippled in a cloudless sky. Above us, the crowd seemed to partition itself into various camps, some singing, some praying, others laughing and laying bets.

Jesus trudged on as if unaware of any of this. It was a fantastic effort to climb the hill. Then Jesus fell a third time. A cough rattled his lungs and he spit blood.

The crowd, which had hurried alongside Jesus, pausing as he paused, groaning as he groaned, doubting as he doubted and exhorting him toward the summit the whole time, stopped. I wondered at these—whether they interpreted some kind of justice in this squalor, derived some sort of satisfaction, or whether they didn't look upon Jesus' tribulations as a foreshadowing of their own, and thus observing hope to forestall their own, thinking, *Yes, this man is condemned as I am condemned, but it shall not be today, not today … and if not today, perhaps not at all! Oh, think not on it!*

A madman ran into the road and helped Jesus to his feet. And he produced a very dirty rag and wiped Jesus' lips, and shouldered the cross while Jesus tore at his robe and cast it aside.

For a moment the strength returned to Jesus and the crowd gazed in awe upon the splendor of his human form: the long curve of his thigh, his heaving chest and sinuous arms. He stood, contrapuntal, like Michelangelo's *David* for long seconds. Then he took the cross and pressed forward, telling in this heroic effort the truth about death, not as some sort of failure, but as victory over life.…

By the time he reached the top, exhaustion had overtaken Jesus once again, and his body seemed to collapse upon itself like a dying star.

The soldiers were about their business now. They lay Jesus body upon the cross and bound his wrists and ankles, and having received special instructions produced three long nails. The one, careful to make a clean job of it, aimed a spike at the center of Jesus' palm and raised a cudgel over his head.

Jesus screamed as the nail pierced his flesh and sank into the beam. The soldier placed a hand over Jesus' mouth.

"Two more," he said, "relax," as they affixed Christ to his cross.

"Now the hard part," the soldier whispered in Jesus' ear. And they hoist the cross upright and dropped it in the hole.

Jesus' shuddered. Vomited. Then seemed to grin as a thin, rust-colored stream ran down his leg.

A portion of the crowd turned away then and began their trek downhill to return to their former lives, such as they were: Sunday supper, *Times* crossword, whatever might suffice until the working week arrived next morning—and feeling as if they had seen something; *tourists,* I'd call them, not interested in much beyond *their* experience of the event.

Some others milled about awhile, satisfied that the threat had subsided; yet vaguely troubled that their satisfaction fell short.

Others succumbed to grief. Still others puzzled over the event, wondering at it, yet no more edified than an animal sniffing at a dead pup.

Jesus panted, trying to catch his breath.

I took Barbara and Mary and the children away and led them the long way to the tomb where Jesus was to be laid.

"Wait here. I shall be with Jesus and comfort him." And I made my way up the back of the hill. There I found a soldier pissing on a sponge, snuck up behind him and broke his neck. Then I donned the uniform and joined the others under the cross.

Jesus was dying now. One by one the organs were shutting down as the blood fled into his brain. His eyes fluttered and he looked down on me. And he thrust his body forward, twisting in the way one might throw off a wrestler. And he laughed a little. Then he gazed upward, then he spit. This sputum, little more than a pink fleck of foam, stuck to the patch of hair beneath his lip, fluttered there a moment, then sailed away on the breeze. And Jesus, seeming finally to catch his breath, let out a long sigh.

Then I heard him calling me from within. "Promise me, Beezy," he said.

"I promise thee, Lord," I said.

He laughed again, little more than a hiccup. And he was silent a long time.

After a while the convulsions started and I took up a spear and placed it beneath Jesus' sternum and listened for a sign. But there was nothing left to hear ... so I pushed the point of the spear, tentatively at first, then in all earnest, into Jesus' chest, piercing the aorta so that a thick black ichor ran down my arms, burning, burning, burning, burning.

Resurrection

After the body was taken down from the cross I took Jesus in my arms and carried him to the secret place where he was to be buried. Mary and the boy were waiting with a group of women in the shadow of the rock. They took Jesus' body from me and made preparations for burial. After washing the body, they rubbed it with balsam and with myrrh and other holy oils know to the women of that area.

As the resins boiled in a little pot held over a fire, I dandles the child on my knee.

"Uncle," Mary spoke to the child and smiled at me.

The child gurgled and kicked his little legs, and he stretched his arms wide as infants do.

One of the women began to keen in ritual mourning.

"No, sister," said Mary loathe to follow a custom. "Neither mourning nor celebration shall attend Jesus' death. As in life, eschew shibboleth. The linen now."

And they wrapped the body in sheets so that it resembled nothing so much as a corpse, as all corpses shall.

"Should we say something," I asked when it was all done.

Mary thought. "No," she said. "Let us each remember Jesus in our own way."

And we placed the body inside the tomb, laying it tenderly upon a slab, and rolled a boulder before the entrance. And then we turned away with a great heaviness in our hearts.

Then Mary, Barbara and the children and I walked out of that country, for truly there was nothing left there. After many days we arrived in the new place, and I made arrangements for a house where Mary and Barbara lived for many years. I looked in on them from time to time. As the child grew into manhood, Mary Magdalene grew frail. As she lay dying I came to the house.

"Once it seemed the whole world lay before us," said Mary, grown wistful. "What happened to that young girl?"

"She became a woman."

"And you, you devil?"

"I've grown old, somehow."

"Promise me, Beezy," she said.

And understanding her heart, I said "I promise you, sister," remembering the young girl that I was once infatuated with.

After the funeral we left for yet another place. On the journey, Jesus' son asked many questions, which I answered the best I could. And when he established himself in the new place, I faded out of his life.

Of course I followed from a distance— watched as this son bore a son, and that bore a son, each Jesus by half, yet possessed of a grace.

You know how it is, my friend, to come upon an old acquaintance you haven't seen in many years;

how seeing this semblance should dredge up those memories of a time when one was possessed of strength, dancing and talking through the night; then turning to the son, who didn't especially want this burden or any another, realize that life follows its own course, neither a continuation of strength, nor its addition, but a redirection?

For a time I fantasized one of these might pick up the cross. Of course that's just fantasy. Just last week, you know, I saw this fellow coming out of a mid-town office building, tie askew, hardly aware of his inheritance, as is only right. And as he ducked into a waiting car, kissed his wife and tossed his briefcase into the back and the car pulled off the curb, I saw a child through the rain-streaked window, who saw me and smiled back.

Thus life follows life, not according to some plan, perhaps, but a deeper pattern inscribed on a gene. And so.

You look to me for a meaning? I give you none.

Amen.